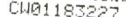

FOXY TALES:

FOXY AND TIGER

By David Head

COPYRIGHT DETAILS

First Paperback Edition 2016

All rights reserved. This book may not be reproduced in any form, in whole or in part, without written permission from the author.

ISBN: 978-1533430496

DEDICATIONS

I would like to thank everyone close to me who helped with this book. 'Tiger' was very supportive and encouraged me to turn a screenplay I wrote which was collecting dust in my desk drawer, into this novel you are reading now. I would also like to thank all involved in creating the illustrations. The illustrations were collaboration with friends and family to make sure that this book really became everyone's book and not just the authors. Thanks also to Christy O'Connor whose Photoshop input gave the cover a nice 'pop'. Last but not least, a big 'thank you' to Christopher Sand-Iverson for his edits.

I hope you enjoy Foxy Tales: Foxy and Tiger (full title) as much as I did writing it.

Contents

1 – THE FOX AND THE HUNTERS 1

2 – THE TOURETTE'S RIDDEN DONKEY 4

3 – WHO'S COMING WITH ME? 8

4 – THE HIPPO WHO THOUGHT HE WAS A DINO 13

5 – THE RUMBLE IN THE JUNGLE – DINO V FOXY 19

6 – ENTER TIGER 29

7 – THE UNWELCOME VISITOR TO THE DEEP JUNGLE......................37

8 - JUST WHAT DOES A TIGER'S CAVE LOOK LIKE ANYWAY? 44

9 - THE SURVEILLANCE MISSION AND STAKE OUT WITH AN EXPLANATION OF FOXISMS..49

10 – THE CONGLOMERATE 68

11 – REFUGE IN THE DEEP JUNGLE..76

12 – THE PREPARATION FOR BATTLE! 83

13 – THE PERIMETER OF THE CONGLOMERATE................................,91

14 – THE BOSS BATTLES IN THE CONGLOMERATE!..........................102

15 – THE CELEBRATION IN THE DEEP JUNGLE 115

1 – THE FOX AND THE HUNTERS

Foxy was frightened.

The Jungle at night time with the pouring rain battering down on the sickly, sloshy mud became his nightmare. Normally for a fox a mud hole is a haven, a prize piece of real estate even, but a mud hole nonetheless. However, on a night like this when you are a fox being pursued by a hunter with a double barrelled shotgun, it is a living hell.

Foxy had been on the run before, scrambling through bushes, evading people, but this time felt different. The sheer thought of that double barrelled shotgun being fired at him was enough to make him give up scavenging for chickens, eggs and scraps for good. Today though was a rare time when Foxy was innocent. This stalking by a predatory hunter was pure sport. Or was it? Something sinister was happening in The Jungle, something was taking over. But for Foxy, he had no time to think about the reason for being chased. He just knew that his life could be coming to an end.

"Keep going, he went this way!" the hunter screamed into the wet jungle night. "Pesky fox, we already destroyed your home. So you better keep on running 'cos we're gonna run all your kind outta here. You hear me, you rodent?" The hunter panted with pure venom and saliva trickled down his moustache. It was a thick, bushy moustache, the kind that if you were to eat soup then you would almost certainly have the remains lodged in your hairs for days to come.

Foxy ran hard. A spectacular sight as he sometimes clipped the ground with all fours, but during full speed his legs were often all off of the ground like a steed devoid of its white knight. Foxy ventured further into The Outer Territories of the forest-like jungle. Only the adrenaline pumping through his torso kept him going. He had been here before, he knew the terrain like the back of his paw but he was tired. The mud and rain had slowed him down but he battled on. The hunters were closing in, and in different circumstances Foxy would be the first to let them know that you cannot outfox a fox.

Foxy ran to an oak tree and stood tall on his hind legs. Well, tall if you count 2 feet 11 inches as tall, but Foxy always knew in life that anyone, regardless of height, could make themselves look big. Could you look big with a double barrelled shotgun in your face? Perhaps not, but now was not the time to test it. Foxy slumped up against the old oak tree exhausted. With whatever strength he had left, he pawed at its door. He tilted his head to the right with force as he heard a click in the bramble over the way. The hunter was getting closer and Foxy accidentally stepped on some loose tree twigs to give up his location. Foxy pawed at the door again and again, but nothing. The hunter had grown livid and was running on pure adrenaline and gaining ground on the fox. There was nothing else for it. Foxy leapt into the air and performed a dive in a vertical motion. If there was a crowd of animals they would have gasped with excitement. As Foxy hit the ground, he burrowed quickly under the mud and took refuge in a hole, a mud hole of course.

Now this hole was a haven to Foxy. It was warm, comfortable and not an ounce of damp on his sandpapery fur. It was quiet too. At least it would have been if not for Foxy's heartbeat. His heart was pumping so fast that it was a mystery that it didn't plough through his rib cage, and if Foxy had more time and space he would certainly have put his paws over his chest to calm it.

The hunter stepped over the area Foxy had dug. Foxy prayed and hoped the hunter would move on. The hunter took a step back and kissed the front of his teeth as the rain drops fell off of his bushy moustache and into the ground below, right where Foxy was. The hunter looked around in frustration.

"Ah hot dang! Nothing. There's nothing here! But you tell 'em fox. You tell em all! I'm coming back and I ain't coming alone! You hear me?" This act of bravado from the human hunter with a weapon that would literally disintegrate an animal into little pieces was lost on Foxy. The hunter walked off stomping into the puddles in the mud in anger with his thick chunky workman's boots.

Foxy burrowed his head out of the ground and coughed a few mouthfuls of mud out, scrambled to his hind legs and performed a shake reminiscent of a dog after it had been swimming in a lake it shouldn't have.

Foxy turned to the oak tree door. It creaked open and Foxy entered.

2 – THE TOURETTE'S RIDDEN DONKEY

The oak tree was Donkey's home, a large floor space with a doorway in the left corner and another doorway at the end leading to a corridor. The corridor was just a large branch extension of the oak tree that lay on the ground. Foxy stared at the house and noted how cosy it looked with its warmth highlighted by some candles in the room. There were a couple of tree stumps in the ground to the right of the room acting as chairs with a level surface of a chopped tree, where the candles were, that would serve as a table between them. To the far side of the room were some uneven wooden shelves that had some empty cans on them. Donkey was a long-time friend of Foxy's and had a shade of blue in his brown fur and his tongue would hang out of the side of his mouth. Donkey nearly always walked on all fours with his head slightly dipped as if he was falling asleep. Donkey and Foxy had been through a lot together. But where Foxy was a scavenger, a general troublemaker and a mischievous fox, Donkey was a lot more grounded in his life. Married with a wife and child, his life was complete.

"Yeuck ecksh horrible," said Foxy standing on his hind paws, pawing himself down from head to paw to get clean. In the warm light of Donkey's home, Foxy's reddish-brown fur and grey stomach glowed in the candle light and his eyes of flame orange and green sparkled like a young boy's marble collection. Foxy's bushy tail was almost the size of Foxy's body with the tip grey in colour. "Thank you, Donkey. I appreciate it. How's the wife and child?" Foxy asked politely.

"Jim! Mrs Donkey ran away with baby Jim! Not come back for a while. I miss him Foxy," replied Donkey.

"Oh yesh. Silly me I forget," said Foxy.

"Jim!" Donkey spat. Foxy had rather carelessly forgotten Donkey's tragic plight. When Foxy asked how the wife and kid were he did not mean it in a literal sense. It was more the sort of automated question that we all ask in life to fill and create conversation. Still it was a bit careless, especially now that Donkey had somehow become a bit slow, or learning impaired for the politically correct among you. Actually, Foxy would describe Donkey as being a few sandwiches short of a picnic. To further add tragedy to Donkey's current predicament, Donkey seemed to have developed a condition known as Tourette's. The Tourette's would cause Donkey to blurt out his son's name at any given moment. The Jungle owl doctor never diagnosed him with Tourette's, just declared him as being obsessed with his son. After all what doting father isn't?

    Donkey was once a very confident alpha donkey. However, a few months back Donkey's wife Jill, another donkey of course, left with their son Jim to get some carrots from the forest jungle and never returned. As is rife in current domesticated life, the couple had seemingly grown apart and yet had given no indication to friends. Foxy never once commented on how Jill or Jim seemed unhappy. The news was quite shocking and hit the local jungle lands with the usual gossiping. The local jackals claimed they saw Jill run off with the local Pony while others commented that Jill and Jim had become pets and worked on a farm with some humans way beyond The Outer Territories. The truth of the matter was, no one knew where they were but agreed they were not coming back.

    Foxy stared at Donkey and felt sorry for his friend. Donkey failed to realise that Jim and Jill would not be coming back. But as all friends do, Foxy comforted him with the usual false hope of lies that only comes from a best friend.

    "Well, maybe they'll be back soon Donkey," Foxy said with about as much belief as an atheist in a Catholic mass, "and if they are I will disappear. I need to lie down. And would you look at my tail?"

    "Foxy tail, dirty Foxy," Donkey mentioned.

"Yesh isn't it? It's gone and lost its volume too. I need to puff it up a bit. May I?"

"Jim!" Donkey nodded. Foxy moved towards the corridor in Donkey's tree house. As Foxy walked along the plush passage he wondered what life would be like if he had his life together like Donkey did, minus the broken family of course. But then again Foxy had no family. Foxy was in awe of the solid oak structure as he approached the doorway and opened it. At the back of the room were two poles of wood standing upright, connected in the middle by two rollers to form a sturdy frame. Just to the right of this structure was a small wheel with a hamster inside. This contraption was an animal equivalent of a wringer or mangle used to press things flat or wring water from them. Foxy positioned himself next to the wringer machine, turned and put his tail through the middle space of the two rollers. Foxy then, standing on his hind legs, used a free leg to tap the hamster's wheel. As he did, the hamster started running at a furious pace and the two rollers rolled over Foxy's tail to wring the water out onto the floor. When he had finished, Foxy's tail was drier than the Sahara desert and had more volume and puffiness than a jungle toad's throat. Foxy was proud of how he looked and smiled to himself and trotted back down the corridor to his friend in the main room.

"Perfect! Donkey, I need to rest now. Is that okay with you?" Foxy asked.

"Jim!" Donkey exclaimed.

Foxy walked into the spare room located at the far left of the main room and found the spare bed. The spare room was just a hollowed out large branch, very little room to move and Foxy noted that this would probably have been Jim's room as he got older. The bed was a slab of wood, uneven but comfortable enough for Foxy. There was a circular cut out just above the bed that allowed a pleasant breeze to enter the room. Foxy slapped the bed softly as if trying puff it up and flopped onto it. He was spent.

Night times are bad for foxes. They often spend their days and nights scavenging for food or sometimes, like today, running for their lives. Tonight was no exception; the events of the hunters chasing him and driving him away from his home had affected him more than he was willing to show Donkey. Foxy suffered from being too confident at times which led others to think he did not need help. But, while asleep, he continually tossed and turned feeling uneasy about the night's events.

"Nooooooooooooooooo!" Foxy screamed, waking up in in a cold sweat and panting like a thirsty dog. Visibly shaken and stirred, Foxy placed his paw on his leg that shook as if a nerve ending had not been shut off. Foxy swung his legs round and placed his paws on the cold floor. He placed his free paw outside of the oak tree house window and let some rain build up and then splashed it on his sweating furry face.

"No more. This has to stop!"

3 – WHO'S COMING WITH ME?

It was morning.

Foxy clambered about outside Donkey's lush oak tree house, pacing up and down. If foxes wore sneakers, Foxy would have worn a hole in them.

"Donkey! Come out here for a second," Foxy ordered Donkey.

"Jim! Is it Jim?" Donkey foolishly asked.

"No, Donkey it's Foxy."

"Yes Foxy?"

"Round up your neighbours, I have a speech I need to make. I have a to-do list longer than the Pink Panther's tail!"

"Jim!"

Donkey ran off and Foxy psyched himself up for Donkey's return.

Donkey reached the tree house, leapt and grabbed a long rope hanging from a bell that was dangling from it. With the rope firmly in his mouth, he began to thrash himself around yelling the word "Jim" through gritted teeth, and the bell created chimes not dissimilar to the chimes at a church wedding.

Instantly, animals of every type came out of the woodwork, the holes, the skies, the clouds - you name it they appeared. Otters, snakes, badgers, rabbits and a huge entourage of animals that you would normally see in a forest appeared. You see, this part of The Jungle is known as The Outer Territories and is situated on the peripheries of The Jungle. As a result of its location, The Outer Territories is more forest than jungle, with animals to match. If you were to travel beyond The Outer Territories, with each step the surroundings would become more jungle, hazardous and have much more menacing and dangerous animals.

After Donkey was finished, he let go of the rope and fell to the ground with a thump, accidentally did a forward roll and ended up at Foxy's feet. He wearily raised his head and winked at Foxy.

"Foxy go now!" Donkey said.

"Thanks Donkey," replied Foxy.

"Jim!" Donkey cried.

Foxy scrambled up onto a tree stump, stood tall on his hind legs and paws and pushed his thick, bushy tail back to address his audience gathered round him. It was as if he was the mayor of the community. Foxy had an idea of what he was about to say and while resting last night, played out his speech over a hundred times in his head. It is very common for all of us to do this. Other people go over in their heads exactly how they are going to portray a situation. However, Foxy should know, as everyone who does this exercise should have known, these things rarely go according to plan or, indeed, how we would like them to.

"My fellow animals," said Foxy as he stood proudly sideways on to his audience, his nose pointing at a forty-five degree angle. Foxy smelled the beautiful forest air and took his time and grew more confident as he waited. Foxy looked out towards his audience sharply. Foxy realised this was a mistake. Foxy should have seen this coming, but then again how could he? He is a fox, a scavenger; he normally had no need to address people in such a manner. All he needed to do was use his cunning, his deceit and lies to get what he wanted. Foxy realised that the events he played over in his head the night before had been foolhardy. He had not even begun his speech and felt he had already lost his audience.

Foxy eyed his audience left to right, and sure enough his confidence had waned. He looked over to Donkey to get some courage and stared. Donkey gawped back at Foxy, but was it admiration or confusion? This is a critical juncture, Foxy thought.

"Oh dang. Come on Foxy," he whispered to himself, "you've been in tougher jams than this, use your Foxisms. The animals love you, they all love you. Unleash some of that foxiness of yours!" Foxy took a gulp and unleashed his mentally prepared speech. "Yesh! My fellow animals." Foxy realised he had left out the insects who scowled back at him. "And insects…" that pleased the insects but upset the bugs, "…and bugs." Yep, that upset the reptiles. "And reptiles," which of course upset the toads. "And… er… amphibians?" At this point Foxy noticed some birds flying in the air. "Fox alive. My fellow everyone. Right, for far too long we've been at the mercy of the man and whatever is going on from beyond our jungle. Well I say… Enough. Enough. And, enough begins now!" Foxy struck his paw into the air to drive home his point, confidence exuding from every paw. Yes that is paw, not pore. "Only yesterday," Foxy continued, "for the fourth time this month, I was evacuated from my hole… I mean my home. Yesh, yesh my home. How is a fox to survive if he has to move from his home every day? Right? You follow me? He can't function like this. I am not special," Foxy emphasised the word special, almost encouraging someone to disagree with him, but was met with vacant stares from the animals in the vicinity. Foxy cleared his throat. "Ahem, I am merely a jungle animal. But together, together with your help I can be special!" This was it. Foxy felt powerful as his mentally prepared speech took shape and had purpose, with confidence exuding from every pore. Yes pore this time not paw. "We can be special!" Foxy continued, "…and we can fight back against the tyranny of the man. Join me and we can put an end to this destructive conflict and rule The Jungle as we rightly should! Yesh!" It should have been a powerful way to end the speech. It had a crescendo of vowels and consonants exciting the crowd, at least in Foxy's head. "Who's coming with me?"

Foxy paused and waited for the expected avalanche of insistence from his peers to join him. It was futile. The expression on Foxy's face had gone from one of confidence to one of uncertainty and confusion. The normally cocky, confident, cheeky and cute fox was at an end. He had no support.

"Jim! I with you Foxy!" Good old Donkey. He never lets Foxy down, does he?

"That's one. Come on animals, who else?" Foxy retorted. Alas, his plea fell on deaf ears. Silence came over them and a ball of tumbleweed rolled into view. The silence was embarrassing and painful to experience and one by one the birds flew off. They were followed by the snakes that slithered off quietly and the rabbits thumped themselves on their way. The final animal to leave was a tortoise, and the tortoise, not exactly the fastest animal alive, took what felt like an eternity before it left Foxy's personal space. Foxy was left with Donkey. Donkey paw punched into the air as if some great miracle had occurred.

"Come on Donkey, these aren't the only animals in The Jungle. Let's go and recruit some," Foxy said with a new surge of confidence, albeit fake confidence. But if Foxy had learnt anything in life, it was that you must fake it to make it.

"Yes let's recruit. Go maybe find Jim on route eh Foxy?" Donkey replied.

"Yesh Donkey. Maybe we will," sighed Foxy.

Hindsight is a terrible thing and Foxy felt bad for sure. But actually, on reflection, Foxy did not do too badly. He may not have got the team that he so desperately needed but he did manage to keep his best friend on board. Sure, it was a cringe filled experience and one that will make him cringe for some time, but tomorrow is another day with new opportunities. Now what on earth was so bad about that? Nothing really, except that Foxy's only recruit was a loyal halfwit.

"Oh well," said Foxy, "one isn't bad I guess." Foxy and Donkey walked off towards The Deep Jungle territories to try and recruit some more able bodied animals.

4 – THE HIPPO WHO THOUGHT HE WAS A DINO

"Who else join us Foxy?" asked Donkey optimistically.

"I don't know Donkey... I really don't know," Foxy answered with a bitter taste in his mouth.

"Just us Foxy! Us against the world!"

"Yesh... just perfect," sighed Foxy. Foxy really had no idea who else would join them. I mean after all what did they have? A small but courageous fox and a Tourette's ridden donkey with the attention span of a goldfish? Like a game of Russian roulette with six bullets and only one player, it did not look good. The fact was the motivational speech that Foxy delivered moments earlier had taken it out of him. He really hoped to do better with his speech, but he had fallen short and the harsh reality had hit him.

Foxy and Donkey moved deeper into The Jungle. They were now quite a distance from Donkey's oak tree estate. With every step they moved deeper into The Jungle where a vast range of animals would certainly reside. The Outer Territories would soon become a distant memory. The couple walked for quite some time and the new terrain was different. Whereas The Outer Territories was plush with green, plants and sometimes undergrowth, this part of The Jungle was a truer jungle - it was hot, and very muddy. Each step that Donkey took made his hooves stick heavily on the thick, muddy and gooey floor. The trees in this part were a lot higher and incredibly dense with leaves. It was a far cry from the forest of The Outer Territories. Every time Foxy looked around he immediately felt out of place. After a few steps Foxy lost all patience.

"Dang this place," said Foxy. "Is there not anyone here?"

"Foxy and Donkey," replied his Tourette's affected pal. The climate had begun to take its toll on Foxy and Donkey. It had got warmer and drier. The air had a muggy feel to it and made Foxy walk with his mouth open gasping for air. Donkey of course walked with his mouth open due to not being the sharpest knife in the drawer. One thing was certain; this area of The Jungle would demand Foxy and Donkey's full attention. Not even Foxy on many of his countless scavenging escapades had encountered terrain like this. They approached a fjord ahead of them. The fjord was not very big, only ten metres in length but there was no way of telling how deep it could be.

"Dang to this. I'm gonna walk right through that mud! Come on Donkey!" Foxy gestured with his paw.

"Jim!"

Foxy stood again on his hind legs and began to wade through the mud. Not far behind Donkey followed but remained on all fours. The mud was up to Foxy's waist and it was touching Donkey's chin.

Suddenly, Foxy went flying through the air and landed four metres ahead face down in the dirty, muddy, sloshy water.

"What the...?" Foxy said somewhat startled.

"Jim!" Donkey screamed in a startled panic.

Neither of them was prepared for what they saw next. Foxy had obviously tripped over something, something large. Sure enough as they both looked into the middle of the fjord, the mud moved left to right and then backwards and forwards. Donkey looked at Foxy, worried with his tongue out covered in mud, and Foxy looked back puzzled. Donkey and Foxy watched the mud as it continued to move and like a cake that was baking it rose higher and higher. As the mud climbed higher and higher, Foxy's eyes widened as a large moving object appeared out of the mud. Donkey gulped when he saw it was large and purple. It was an awesome sight with a weight approximately two thousand pounds and over eight feet in height and fat as anything. The mud dripped slowly off of the living mass object and revealed a large head, with big round eyes and nostrils like car headlamps. Attached to the large head was a round body with rough skin and four legs protruding out with hooves, not paws. It was a large animal for sure, but Foxy and Donkey had no idea who or what it was.

"ARROOOOOOOOOOOOOOOAAAAAAAAAHHHHHHH!" The large animal shouted rather like a tyrannosaurus rex dinosaur. The roar was obviously faked for effect, but it worked in startling both Donkey and Foxy.

"My god! What is it?" Foxy asked.
"Not Jim! Jim!" Donkey unhelpfully replied.
"Yesh Donkey, it certainly isn't Jim!"
Suddenly, the animal again spoke with a fake roar and a voice that was gruff and rough as if the animal had been chewing on leather gloves.
"I am Dino. Lord Of The Hippos!" The animal said, revealed now as a hippopotamus.
"He's gone feral!" Foxy exclaimed.

"State your business! Who disturbs Dino's beauty mud bath? Answer me!"

Foxy stood up and wiped away the mud from his face and nose using his tail as if it were a stiff broom.

"Sorry dear chap. Did not mean to disturb," Foxy said with some charm in his voice.

"I thought you were one of those pesky humans come to destroy my home!" Dino said.

"I can assure you that that could not be further from my mind. We will be on our way…"

"Jim!"

Donkey, normally being a bit slow was on this occasion way ahead of Foxy. Why on earth would they want to get on their way? Could this big tub of lard be exactly what Foxy needed on his adventure? Foxy paused in his tracks.

"Hang on a minute. Dino?"

"Yes?" Dino replied.

"Allow me to introduce myself. I am Foxy… er… Lord Of The Foxes. And this is Donkey Lord Of The Halfwits, I mean Donkeys."

"Jim!" Foxy raised his paw to cover Donkey's mouth.

"Don't mind him Dino, we think he's got Tourette's you know," Foxy joked.

"I see." Dino said perplexed.

"Anyway I digress…" Foxy said.

"GRAAARRRROOOOO!" Dino again roared a dramatic dinosaur type growl.

"Yesh well…" Foxy continued, "…listen, we are on a mission to recruit… recruits in our gang to go and battle the humans to get them off of our turf. Now I know it is a lot to ask but we could do with a big strong lad like you on our merry mission?"

"Dino say yes! Yes! Have you noticed I am big but extremely fit and lean?"

"Yes!" Donkey for once responded with just the right thing to say and his stupidity saved them. Dino was about as trim as a well fed wild boar, something Foxy picked up on worried that Donkey would scare him off.

"Don't take the mick Donkey. I know he's the fattest thing ever but we need him. Yesh, he is the fattest thing I have ever seen and I have been on safari…" Foxy whispered, causing Dino to butt straight back in.

"I am so trim and it's all down to this vegetarian diet I am doing. Meat? Meat is for wimps. I like grass. If you two out of shape, puny things stuck to my diet you could look just like me. Come on let's be on our way."

"Back of the net! Let's go Donkey," Foxy excitedly said.

"Donkey go. Jim!" Donkey cried.

The gang got no more than two steps when Dino stopped dead in his tracks.

"What is it?" Foxy asked.

"What is it? My internal body clock is telling me that now it's my time to sleep. I have been up for one whole hour today, Dino needs his beauty sleep, don't you know?" Dino said.

"Is this a joke?" Foxy asked.

"No," replied Dino.

"Dino, what about your new fitness regime?" Foxy lowered the tone of his voice to a whisper and blurted out a Foxism, "those fat legs make an elephant's look like a sparrow's." Foxy focused his attention back to Dino. "What're you on about?"

"Dino move for no one," said Dino with a stubborn look on his face.

"You're afraid," countered Foxy trying to trick Dino to come along.

"What?" Dino asked somewhat insulted.

"You want to stay and hide you coward!" Foxy cried. Foxy was sincere in his response and could not understand Dino's need to sleep seeing as that is what he was doing not long ago. However, the accusation filled Dino full of anger. Dino stood up and was absolutely enormous. He blew air out at Foxy that forced him back a few steps.

"Groooooowwwwlllllll. Puny fox. I will crush you now," Dino shouted which sent Foxy flying back a few metres. Donkey trembled with fear. "I will see you in the ring!" Dino roared.

"The ring?" Foxy asked.

"The Jungle Boxing Ring of course!"

"What?"

"Dino makes puny fox a deal. If I win I stay and have my beauty sleep. If you win I go with you as your soldier, puny fox."

"No," appealed Foxy, his manipulation tactics for once backfiring. A flood of thoughts came into Foxy's mind. Was this hippopotamus really challenging him to a fight? How on earth could that be an even contest?

"Hahahaha who is the coward now?" The accusation had done little to change Foxy's mood but for some reason stirred something up inside Donkey.

"Foxy afraid of no one. He accepts Dino challenge! Jim! Jim!" Donkey cried and winked at foxy.

"Oh crumbs!" Foxy exclaimed, aware of the ordeal that lay ahead of him. Foxy swallowed hard and began to plan how he could use his cunning to get out of this situation unscathed.

5 – THE RUMBLE IN THE JUNGLE – DINO V FOXY

Animals surrounded the square circle. A square circle is what is known as a boxing ring. The boxing ring in this jungle was not dissimilar to a human conventional boxing ring albeit with a few jungle modifications. On a normal boxing ring you have four iron posts, one in each corner of the square. In this jungle boxing ring, some animals had simply used four tree stumps of varying length and placed one in each corner. The normal four ropes that tie around the posts to enclose the combatants in a conventional boxing ring were replaced with long thinner tree twigs, the kind that Tarzan would probably swing from. That left the mattress. Naturally, being a jungle there was no mattress here, just the usual uneven floor made of dried mud with some sand and shingle.

Around the squared circle stood the habitants of this part of The Jungle including a rather curious snake with a cone shaped sea shell wrapped into his tail. Right next to the square circle was a hollow log overturned and behind it three unoccupied cut down tree stumps, reserved for the judges at ringside.

What of the contents of the ring? Well, in one corner, what they would refer to in normal boxing as the blue corner, you had Dino. Dino stood with a small cloth round his waist, quite a ridiculous sight as the self-proclaimed trim Dino was nothing of the sort. Dino's tummy was hanging over the cloth making him look like a muffin where the top hangs over the bottom. On second look one would be forgiven for thinking Dino looked like a big baby. Actually he looked like a ridiculous purple sumo wrestler.

If the sight of Dino was ridiculous, then nothing prepared the audience for what stood in the red corner. Foxy waited on his hind legs with a pair of blue shorts and white stripes down either side almost obscured by large boxing gloves over his fists, or paws if you will. Where on earth the animals got such items from is a mystery.

The curious snake, called Snake slithered to the centre of the ring. Snake patted the sea shell cone that doubled up as a microphone that he was holding with his head. As he did this, the gathering of animals slowly lowered their volume to the point you could almost hear a pin drop in The Jungle.

"Welcome boxxxxxxing fans! Come witneessssss the might of thesssse two stallionsss asss they battle it out for gloating rightsssss and bragging rightssss. Whoo!" The snake's delivery of the introduction was both exciting, creepy, seductive and met with a huge roaring cheer from all the animals. "In the blue corner," continued Snake, "weighing in at a trim two thoussssand and forty five poundsssss and a height of eight feet ten inchesss from the unknown Jungle of The Beyond Territory... Dinooooo The Desssssssstroyerrrrrrrr!" The Snake slithered over to Dino and whipped his tail out with the sea shell wrapped in it and positioned it right near Dino's large gaping mouth.

"ARRRRROOOOOOOOOOOOOOOOOOOOOOOOOOOOOOO OOOOOOOOOOOOOOOOOOOOOOOOOOOOOOAAAAAAAAAAAA AAAAAAAAAAAAAAAAAAAAAAAAHHHHHHHHHHHHHHHHH HHHHHHHHHHHHHHHHHHHHHH!" Dino screamed with such ferocity that a tidal wave of air like a sonic boom went over the ring and into the crowd, blowing many of the smaller animals like the rabbits back a few dozen rows.

Meanwhile, Foxy was bobbing up and down, shifting the weight from one paw to the other concentrating on his own business.

"And hissss opponent. From the slummssssssssssssssss..." Snake emphasised the 's' in slums. This did not go unnoticed by Foxy who narrowed his eyes and let out a huff. "The garbage binssssss, the dirt, the dump, the coldesssssst mosssst dissssssssgussssssting vile placesssss on earth," Snake said with disgust.

"Easy Snake, come on!" Foxy appealed to no avail as Snake continued.

"The rankesssst disgusssssting holessss of The Outer Territory and beyond. Weighing in at forty five poundsssss at a height of two feet eleven inchesssss. Fooxxxxxxxxy The Foxxxxxxx!!!" A rather lacklustre delivery from the snake as he whipped his tail Foxy's way with the cone wrapped up in it.

In what seemed like an eternity Foxy stared at the cone, unsure what to say. Foxy cleared his throat and opened his mouth. When nothing but warm air came out, Foxy closed his mouth again and just gritted his teeth.

"Grrrrrrrrrrr?" Foxy asked. The response from the crowd was not enthusiastic, just a meaningless silence.

"Lettssssssss get readyyyy to rumblllleeeeeeeeeeeeeeeeee!" Snake proclaimed and slithered with lightning speed to a bell sat perched on the hollow overturned tree, and whipped it with his tail to make a loud Ding noise to indicate the first round.

Foxy turned around and looked towards Dino. Foxy's focus was momentarily distracted by the entry of a pig clambering through the ropes into the squared circle. It was a female pig, short and fat bizarrely wearing a white and black pinstripe shirt. Where did the pig get a referee's attire from in The Jungle? No idea, your guess is as good as mine, but it was somewhat fitting for the upcoming fight and looked like a rag that had been treated with some dark food colouring like berries to create the dark stripes.

"Alright. Oink, oink," the pig chortled. "I wanna clean fight oink. Okay? No messing around. Oink, touch yer gloves and go!" Pig motioned with her hooves and smashed them together to make a 'chink' noise not far from the noise champagne glasses make. The fight was on.

Dino slowly walked out to the centre of the ring. In the other corner Foxy quickly, but apprehensively, walked out.

"Puny, wimpy little fox!" Dino snarled at Foxy and extended his long thick arms, or are they legs? Dino used his tree trunk legs with fat hooves covered in huge boxing gloves to push Foxy back a few feet.

"Gulp!" Foxy gasped. Dino lunged a jab at Foxy that landed flush on his jaw and sent him flying into the turnbuckle from where he started. The turnbuckle in a boxing ring is another name for the corner. As Foxy hit the turnbuckle, he felt the ligaments in his neck tighten and his whole body went erect as if he had heightened senses.

In Foxy's corner, on the outside was Donkey. The Tourette's ridden Donkey, oblivious to the pain Foxy was in, encouraged him as best as he could.

"Fun Foxy fun! Go go go!" Donkey exclaimed. Foxy could hear Donkey clearly as the brute force of Dino's jabs sent him back. Foxy was now in a perfect position to respond and correct the stupid but harmless Donkey.

"Yesh, it is fun Donkey, but not when you are being hit by something that's as large as a hippo!" Foxy retorted. Foxy had little time for conversation as Dino ploughed forward towards Foxy, the once sloth-like walk of Dino was now alarmingly fast and agile.

Dino let out a war cry. Despite the newfound speed of Dino, Foxy was still light years ahead of him in terms of pace and casually moved out of the way which sent Dino spiralling head first into the turnbuckle.

Suddenly, Foxy rotated his tail at a dizzying pace which momentarily gave him flight. With his hind legs off of the floor Foxy pummelled Dino's stomach with some punches of his own. However, Foxy had not thought about Dino's worryingly high level of body fat as he made repeated contact with Dino's flabby stomach. Dino's stomach rippled like someone lifting up a carpet many times and shaking it out.

Dino let out a laugh. "Dino strong! Feel my muscles fox!" Dino punched Foxy with a hard right.

"Yikes!" Foxy cried.

During this rather one sided affair, the commentary from Snake had not ceased. Snake was still clutching his sea shell in his tail and informing the gathered audience of animals just what was happening, presumably for those in the cheap 'seats'.

"OOOOh that one hurtsssss Foxxxxxy," reported Snake. "It'ssssss like a human basssssketball out there!" Snake was not kidding, Dino had Foxy curled up into a ball and was patting him to the floor. Every time Foxy bounced up off the floor, Dino sent him crashing back down with a pat. It was reminiscent of something you would see in a children's cartoon. Dino did not stop there though. He was tired of patting Foxy around, so he picked him up, still curled in a ball and threw Foxy into the air as if he was taking a shot with a basketball. A huge 'swoosh' noise came from the crowd and Foxy went crashing face first into the ground.

"Nothing but net! Swisssssssshhhhhh! Deux Poisssssssss!" Snake commented as Foxy groggily got up. "Here comesssss Dino on the charge. Foxy better get out of the way or he'ssssss gonaaa..." Snake never finished his sentence. Instead his sentence was ended by the sight of Foxy again going flying across the ring. "Yesssss, thatssss what I wasssss afraid of," the snake confirmed. As Foxy laid down, the pig came over to start a count.

"Oink, one, oink, two, oink three," said the pig counting Foxy on the ground. Foxy got up at the count of eight and stood on his hind paws tired. Dino sensed the end was nigh and charged towards Foxy. Whether it was instinct or just blind luck, Foxy managed to get out of the way just in time and his bushy tail caught Dino slightly on the nose. The fur of Foxy seemed to cause an allergic reaction with Dino as he brought his hooves to his large nostrils and his cheeks reddened.

"AHHHH CHOOO!" Dino screamed as he sneezed and then shook his head. Dino's face was red from embarrassment and anger. He was about to charge at Foxy but Snake whipped the bell on the outside of the ring to signal the end of the first round.

Foxy slumped in the red corner for the interval of the round. He was spent, his luxurious fur once a desired piece of cloth for some rich aristocrats would be lucky to fetch fifty pounds down a flea market. It was bathed in sweat. It was probably very smelly too. Donkey entered the ring carrying a pale of water in his mouth and tilted his head so the water would run over Foxy. The drops of water cooled Foxy and woke him up, and dripped onto the floor. Foxy's eyes became alive and he raised his paw and threw it onto the floor.

"No, no, no. No more. Foxy says no more Mister Nice Fox. My tail is the key, he did not like the scent of my Foxy tail." Rejuvenation set in on Foxy's previously withered frame, inside him was a warm glowing feeling that was ready to explode, he turned his head directly to Donkey.

"Jim is back." Yep, Donkey completely missed the point yet again.

"No Donkey I'm..." Foxy explained but one look into Donkey's eyes made Foxy realise that explaining was futile. It would be a bit like trying to blow out a light bulb. "Look, just give me some more water will you?" Foxy received the water again on his head and got up.

Ding! The sound from Snake's tail started the second round. Snake started to motion to the crowd of animals getting them hyped up for the upcoming round.

"Puny fox, if I was not a vegetarian you would now be in my belly!" Dino gloated.

"No chance fat hippo," replied the cocky fox.

"This is muscle," said Dino.

"Yeah right, and my tail is bald!" Foxy replied and threw his obviously hirsute tail in front of him. It had the desired effect as Dino again started to sneeze uncontrollably and saw red before he charged with a punch. The punch missed by a mile as Foxy side stepped and used Dino's momentum to throw him into the ropes.

"Great move by Foxxxxy! Dino does not know what hasssss hit him. There looksssss to be ssssomething wrong with Dino'ssss breathing. What will Foxxxxy do now?" Snake was getting excited and finally seeing the potential in Foxy and egging the audience on.

Foxy followed and grabbed Dino's comedic towel pants and yanked them high up and over Dino's head. The crowd of animals laughed, embarrassing Dino further.

"Parentssss if your cubsssss or whatever are watching thisssss, cover their eyessss!" warned Snake as Foxy started to jump from each side of the squared circle off of the ropes like an acrobat. First, he jumped off the rope and bounced towards Dino, then back to the rope and then to Dino. Each time he reached Dino he landed a punch right on Dino's big fat head and a whiff of his tail right under Dino's gaping nostrils..

"Oh Dino'ssss in trouble!" Snake said as all the animals gasped with excitement. "If he'ssss not careful he could go here."

"That's right, come on! FOXXXXXXYY POWEEERRR!" Foxy screamed as he leapt into the air, whipped out his tail at such a ferocious pace that everything appeared to go in slow motion. The wide arc of the tail came around and smacked Dino clean on the chin. The golden light of day glistened as the tail moved forming sparkles of debris in the air.

"OOOOOh that got him!" Snake exclaimed. Dino went flying into the air and let out a huge roar and sneeze as he flew up and then at the height of his ascent, he stopped and fell down. Snake realised what was happening and warned everyone to get back and out of the way.

As Dino landed on the matt of the ring, the entire ring exploded due to the weight and pressure of Dino. Smoke appeared all around making it impossible to see.

For a while the whole jungle was silent, there was nothing happening. The smoke gradually cleared and Snake was the first to be seen as he slithered along the ground asking himself what had happened.

Gradually more and more smoke cleared. The next figure to be seen was Foxy. Cocky Foxy stood there in the centre of the ring with smoke around his right leg. His right leg stood on something obscured by the smoke. The smoke cleared to reveal Dino under his foot. Dino was defeated and baby birds flew around his head.

"Foxy power," Foxy said as the snake writhed and slithered towards Foxy with the sea shell firmly entwined in his tail.

"What a finale! The underdog hasss done it and with it he getsss bragging rightsssss. Let'sssss interview thissss courageoussssss foxxxx." Snake whipped his tail within an inch of Foxy's face.

"Never underestimate me!" Foxy warned. "I told him he couldn't do it. You only brought him in here to bash me up…" Foxy proclaimed in a state of euphoria as Donkey was about to butt in.

"Foxy…" Donkey said.

"Nah nah nah let me finish!" Foxy ordered.

"Jim! Mission!"

"Oh yesh. The mission. Yesh the mission yesh. Snake I want Dino to come with us. This is merely the beginning. We are going through this jungle to make it a better place. So I say this. Dino, come with us we need you." Dino listened to the speech and got up off the floor and shook his head to clear away the proverbial cobwebs. Foxy extended his paw. Dino looked at it and then looked into Foxy's marble coloured eyes and then back to the paw. Dino extended his hoof and they shook hoof and paw.

"You're on," Dino responded. Snake slithered in the middle of them and spoke into his sea shell.

"What an end to the contesssst fantasssstic. Ssssssee you nexxxxt time!" Snake looked like he was about to continue before Dino stepped in front of Snake and told him to shut up.

A little later Foxy, Donkey and Dino walked along deeper into The Jungle.

"What's the plan Foxy?" Dino asked.

"We need another recruit, someone else, a powerful person," Foxy said with a cocked paw in the air.

"Huh?" Dino said inquisitively. "What about me?"

"I mean another powerful person Dino, someone in addition."

"Oh okay."

"Jim!" Donkey said, his Tourette's getting the better of him.

"Who is Jim?" Dino asked as Foxy brought his paw to his face and rolled his eyes.

"Nice one Dino, you just had to ask didn't you?"

"Jim is my boy. Look at Jim. Jim! The best Donkey in the world," Donkey said proudly.

"They've gone haven't they Donkey? We will find them." Foxy assured him with a paw placed on his back.

"Yes Jim! Jim!" Donkey jumped up and down with excitement.

"But we need help," said Foxy.

"There's only one animal that we need," said Dino, "the rest will then follow." Foxy stopped dead in his tracks and looked at Dino wide eyed.

"Who?" Foxy asked.

"Tiger," replied Dino.

"Tiger?"

"Yes we need Tiger."

"Great! Where is he?"

"Tiger is in these parts this way." Dino motioned his hoof in a northward direction. The trio walked off towards a dark path in The Jungle that would lead them into the heart of The Deep Jungle.

6 – ENTER TIGER

As Foxy, Dino and Donkey entered The Deep Jungle they all noticed that it had got hotter, but the prospect of another recruit was making Foxy giddy. The temperature in the area was making it difficult to breathe. Foxy had his tongue out panting in an effort to cool down. Donkey started to flinch more than the Tourette's had made him do before, and Dino's skin was in dire need of some mud to smooth out the cracks.

The Jungle had darkened somewhat and the hot weather was humid and muggy. Foxy could feel the moisture on his fur from the heat and gradually the fading sun was beginning to disappear through the tall trees hanging overhead. Very soon The Jungle would become denser, darker and hotter.

The Deep Jungle was only for the most ferocious of animals and Foxy was alert and walking on all fours sniffing, in between panting for air. Donkey was trembling from nerves and Dino was, well Dino was just Dino.

"Donkey is scared Foxy," whispered Donkey. Foxy looked back at him.

"It's okay Donkey. It'll be alright," assured Foxy with a see through act of bravado. Donkey gulped.

"You realise that Tiger could be anywhere? I only know that Tiger lives in these parts," Dino said.

"Yesh but I've found all kinds of things as a scavenger. I've discovered a scent of nothing I've smelt before. Must be this way." Foxy pointed his head in a northward direction which led through a narrow corridor of high trees into the sky. Gradually, the area brightened. It was quiet, not even a cricket or insect noise could be heard.

"Foxy?" Donkey asked.

"What?"

"Donkey really scared," Donkey stopped in his tracks. Foxy looked back towards Donkey and skipped up close to him.

"Donkey, you love your home right?" Foxy whispered. Donkey gingerly nodded back. "Well if we don't do this soon, we ain't gonna have a home anymore. Understand?" Foxy said.

"But Jim?"

"Jim will have nowhere to live if we don't do this. Trust me on this. Alright my friend?" Donkey nodded as a moment of calm came over him. Dino noticed the temperature had dramatically increased and was showing signs of fatigue.

"It's getting very hot," said Foxy. It was blisteringly hot and even Dino who likes the heat, was walking lethargically.

"Yeah. Habitat of a Tiger. Quite a difference. Even the mud here is hot. I'd have to get used to it if I was to bathe here," replied Dino.

Suddenly Dino stopped dead in his tracks, startled, his nostrils pushed forward and up into the humid air.

"Yesh, I picked that up with my nose too Dino, what is it?" Foxy asked.

"Must be Tiger," replied Dino.

The narrow corridor of The Jungle was beginning to widen out and at the end was a large oval clearing that went off into the distance with trees at the end. The whole clearing was obscured by bushes.

"Okay, be quiet we're here. Tiger must be here. I can sense he's here." Foxy squinted and looked through the bushes studying the clearing ahead. The trio were lying behind the bushes out of sight, there was no noise and no leaves were moving. Out in the clearing was a large layer of water and to the sides some mud and beyond that some leaves on The Jungle plants. Foxy calmed himself down but got distracted by a noise over his shoulder. Foxy turned and saw Donkey's teeth chattering together uncontrollably. "Calm down Donkey!" Foxy ordered.

"Tiger," said Dino and pointed into the clearing somewhere.

"Yesh," Foxy answered as he looked to where Dino was pointing. He could see the tiger.

"Look," Dino chimed in.

"Yesh," Foxy said again, "Beautiful," he added. Dino looked at Foxy.

"Haha. Foxy likes?" Dino laughed.

"What're you on about?" Foxy asked.

"Tiger," Dino replied.

"You're mad, Look! That's a tigress. I was expecting a tiger!" Foxy exclaimed.

"Sorry Foxy. Didn't I mention Tiger was a tigress?" Dino asked.

"No! You certainly didn't. It makes no sense Dino, when I think about it. I would've found out eventually. Remember you cannot outfox a fox," Foxy proudly said. "I want a strong male, not a tigress!"

"Yes. But Foxy, do not call her Tigress, she insists on being called Tiger," warned Dino.

"Why?"

"Women's liberation, political correctness. It's a modern thing. And anyway she is the most ferocious animal in this jungle, male or female. You know what I mean?" Dino looked at Foxy whose gaze was met with a roll of the eyes from Foxy before he went back to admiring the powerful Tiger move. Tiger moved like she had to move for no one. She had an amazing gait and flow, heel to paw, heel to paw. She was elegant, classy but downright ferocious. She had the usual tiger stripes all down her body and the flow of orange met the white and black markings perfectly. Tiger was obviously hot even in her own climate, and walked a bit further into the clearing into a pond filled with beautiful clear water. As she got in she immediately cooled and moved around slightly. After a short time she exited the water and moved around a bit more.

"Yesh, yesh okay. But look at her move... so graceful, stunning. She's a fox alright," admired Foxy.

"She's a tiger," Dino corrected.

"I mean she's beautiful Dino."

"You're a fox."

"I'm also red blooded dang it. Look at those eyes... so soft, large and gentle," Foxy said almost in a hypnotic state. Tiger's eyes were indeed unique, a piercing blue that could cut a hole in the most sky blue of skies.

"You're weird Foxy."

"Shoosh you idiot! You will scare her away. We're here on a mission remember. Now pipe down Dino. Now where'd she go?"

Silence. There was no sign of Tiger as she casually strolled amongst some bushes out of view of the trio watching her.

"Gone," said Dino.

"Just like Jim!" Donkey replied.

"You two halfwits must have scared her off! Well done both of you!" Foxy angrily said.

"What?" Dino innocently replied.

"Ribbing me about Tiger and now she's gone. How will we ever find her now?"

"Maybe she's onto us and will find us and eat us just for fun."

"Don't be daft. In all my years as a fox I have learnt not to be afraid, they can smell fear. I've been in tighter situations than this and besides she don't scare me. No Sir," Foxy confidently said.

Looking back now, Foxy's speech about not being afraid was signposted for what would happen next. It was inevitable really that Foxy would be made to eat his words. As the trio looked beyond to where Tiger once was, it was still hot and quiet. Painfully quiet. None of them heard a thing until Tiger decided to make her presence known in awesome fashion.

Tiger jumped in front of the trio. She must have jumped from somewhere in the trees or at least from higher ground and landed right in front of them. She let out an almighty roar creating an incredible hairdryer effect on the three friends as the hair on their faces went flying back. Tiger was showing her large canines, teeth of a jungle predator. They were huge like cut diamonds with a sparkle coming from the saliva that had caught on the teeth. Had Foxy had any time to think during this show of aggression, he would have noted that this look for Tiger was quite a contrast to the graceful presence just witnessed in the clearing. If Foxy had had any doubts about Tiger's suitability for the team, they had been quashed.

Foxy and the trio jumped out of their skin and cowered together. Even Dino, a larger creature than Tiger was trembling like a schoolboy waiting to be caned. More curious than this though was what lay on Tiger's shoulder. Perched delicately on her shoulder was a crow, with one eye. The crow was jet black in colour as if he had been dipped in some tar used to lay fresh roads and it had a missing eye replaced with a fine slit or scar where the upper and lower eyelids had healed.

"Yikes!" Foxy screamed.

"Jim!" Donkey added.

"Yarrrghh," screamed Dino. Tiger made herself large by stretching out and the sinew of muscle in her legs started pulsing out making her look more authoritative and menacing.

"State your business!" Tiger shouted. Foxy looked at her still dumbstruck and opened his mouth.

"I'm a fox... I scavenge... I generally become a nuisance... I..." Foxy's sentence was cut off by a roar from Tiger. The roar was not as powerful as the roar she used to introduce herself but it still frightened Foxy.

"One more chance fox. What are you doing in my part of The Jungle?" she said.

"Tell her Foxy!" Dino added, which caused Tiger to spin her head toward Dino making him cower even more that he had previously.

"Quiet hippo! I haven't eaten today. Be still or be eaten!" Dino lifted his hoof to his mouth and did a sideways motion mimicking a zip like action. Foxy composed himself and stepped in to try and smooth things over.

"Okay. Okay, everyone relax. Okay, now Tiger let me introduce myself," Foxy walked over to Tiger acting cool, relaxed, cocky and lifted his paw before placing it gently on top of hers in an effort to charm the tigress. "You see we're on a mission, a mission to rid our jungle of the human hunters. To do so, we need your help to join..." Tiger squeezed Foxy's paw very tightly. The force of the squeeze eased Foxy's grip on her paw and made him pull a face as if he had just sucked a lemon. Very painful indeed. "Grrr, I mean lead. Yesh lead our team of men." Tiger looked annoyed at the reference to men. "I mean women ..." Foxy further insulted Tiger and not being sure what to say he finished with, "I mean our group! Yesh, our group." Tiger threw his paw away and Foxy placed his paw into his mouth to suck it to take the pain away and then waved it in the air.

"Nonsense. There are no hunters in this part of The Jungle. My jungle. They would not dare," Tiger confidently said whilst looking into the dense, warm air.

"Be that as it may Tigress," Foxy slapped his head realising he had offended her again by calling her Tigress. "I mean Tiger, I started off at The Outer Territory. Slowly, bit by bit they've pushed me back. It's only a matter of time before they come here and steal your home too."

Tiger rocked her head back hard and laughed into the air harshly. It was a very deep powerful laugh.

"Do you really think a human hunter is any match for a tiger? Foolish Fox," Tiger replied. Tiger had a good point. What could a minor human do to this powerful, fearless Tiger and her entourage? It made Foxy think for a bit, but he was adamant that such a danger exists and had experienced it his whole life on the many dangerous missions he had been on. "Foolish fox," she repeated as if to underline how foolish she believed the courageous fox to be.

"Foxy," said Foxy correcting Tiger in an attempt to be taken more seriously.

"I beg your pardon," she replied looking for a hint of sarcasm in Foxy.

"His name is Foxy," butted in Donkey quite clearly mistaking Tiger's rhetorical question.

"Grrraaaawwwl!" Tiger screamed.

"Gulp," said Donkey.

"Tiger. I'm Foxy, here's Donkey and Dino."

"Enough! I grow tired of such shenanigans. You don't even know who the enemy is."

"With your help…"

"Be gone. Leave. Out of respect for you managing to navigate in here, I will let you leave. But, if you come around here again I'll have myself a nice fox curry. Now Go!"

"Oh so you're an Indian Tiger?" Foxy said and added a wink for good measure. Tiger was not amused and gave Foxy an angry look on her face and let out a 'grmmm' noise. It was enough to bring Foxy crashing back down to earth. "Gulp! We bid you farewell then, Tiger." Foxy stretched his arms out wide holding Donkey and Dino behind him and proceeded to take a step backwards, then another and another before slowly disappearing from Tiger's field of view.

As they wondered out of Tiger's sight, she turned on her heels and strolled off with the elegance the trio had first seen in her. She paused and looked to her shoulder where Crow perched. She looked angry and Crow looked back at her.

"Foolish Foxy," she said.

"Squarrrrrk," agreed Crow. Tiger nodded, turned and made her way back into the clearing. Crow stayed on her shoulder as they both disappeared.

7 – THE UNWELCOME VISITOR TO THE DEEP JUNGLE

It had been quite an eventful day for Foxy, a day filled with more ups and downs than a rollercoaster. Having started well with good intentions to get recruits for his mission, he had an amazing high getting Dino on board only to be brought down to a crashing halt with Tiger's refusal to help.

The trio walked back down the hot, humid narrow path from where they came. Foxy, Donkey and Dino noticed the sky was turning greyer as the humidity eased off. True, they were not far from the opening where they met Tiger, but they were just far enough to notice a climate change. The sky once wet with humidity, was starting to rain a bit and formed puddles in the mud. As the rain hit the puddles it created delicate splashes in unpredictable patterns.

"Well that didn't go well," said Dino. "That didn't quite go according to plan now did it Foxy?"

"No," replied Foxy. "It certainly didn't," he said with regret in his voice, disappointed not to be getting Tiger involved. It would have been amazing to get Tiger on board, Foxy thought. She would certainly have had a lot of pull in The Deep Jungle community. Foxy knew that he now had to find another recruit and after feeling sorry for himself, snapped himself back into the reality. "You know what?" Foxy cried, "She's not the only tiger around here. Guess what we'll do? Forget her. We'll get ourselves a lion, the King of The Jungle. She's all mouth and no trousers that one."

"Tiger wears not trousers Foxy," replied Donkey innocently.

Foxy sighed, "I know Donkey. I know."

The three companions could only have gone a few more steps when something terrible happened. A flash of light appeared accompanied by a crack of light, a very quick loud noise and then a horrific smell. This was a smell Foxy had encountered before. Even though it happened so quickly, Foxy knew exactly what was going on as his heightened senses kicked in and he waited for the confirmation of the smell. It was gunpowder, someone had taken a shot at them.

"Get down!" Foxy shouted. Foxy dived forward through some bushes and took refuge behind a log. He was followed by Donkey who scrambled his way over, then Dino who seemed to just buckle straight forward making a huge dent in the mud on the other side of the log.

"Jim! Foxy, what is?" Donkey asked very confused.

"Hunter," Foxy replied keeping low behind the log. "Why did I not smell his trail?" Foxy said worried, concerned that a hunter got the drop on them. Maybe the sudden and quick climate change had disoriented the once alert fox? "Dino you okay?" Foxy asked.

No reply from Dino. Foxy feared the worst and screamed Dino's name a second time.

"It's okay Foxy," replied Dino. "It's merely a flesh wound." Dino had been hit. A few pellets from the shotgun blast had penetrated Dino's thick skin. There was blood trickling from his shoulder down towards his hoof. It looks worse than it is, Foxy thought.

"Come here, let me see it." Foxy examined it further. "A few pellets from the shotgun blast. You'll be alright. Your lean muscle mass has saved you," Foxy smiled and Dino smiled back at Foxy.

"Dino power Foxy!" Dino replied.

"Yesh," replied Foxy. Foxy was still not sure where the blast came from or from who. He had assumed it was a hunter. It had to be a hunter, but this far out? Even Tiger said with some certainty they would not reach this far, but Foxy always suspected it.

Foxy lifted his head slightly above the log and peered over through narrowed eyes. He tracked his eyes and head from left to right, looking outward into the slightly wet ground and greyish sky. Suddenly Foxy stopped and saw the hunter about thirty metres to the northwest. There he is. I have seen him before Foxy thought. It was the same hunter that had chased him to within an inch of his life the day before. The same hunter with the ridiculous bushy moustache that probably had this morning's breakfast still stuck in it. Foxy would never forget a hunter and this one walked with his gun held erect and a finger ready on the trigger to strike.

"Dang," sighed Foxy. "Yesh, it's that hunter alright. The same one that chased me out of the woods," he thought for a moment and then came up with an idea. "It's me he wants. You two make a run for it and I will lead him up that hill to the higher ground."

"No Foxy," replied Donkey concerned, for once fully aware the seriousness of the situation and unwilling to leave his friend.

"Donkey, go. I'll be back. Look after Dino. Go. Go. Go!" Foxy ordered.

Seconds later, Donkey and Dino rolled backwards through bramble and down the hill. The momentum of the hill kept them going at quite a pace. Foxy braced himself to move and held his paws on the log, soggy from the rain, and pushed himself up and down with his front paws ready to pounce out when he had courage. On the count of three Foxy thought, then realised that he was perhaps analysing too much and must move now or his friends would get hurt.

Foxy leapt out. As soon as he cleared the log, the familiar noise of the gun with the flash of light came. The pellets of the shotgun blast battered into the log making sawdust of it. As he moved away from danger, Foxy accelerated rapidly as another shot narrowly missed him.

"I got you... you son of a," cried the hunter spewing venom and hatred with every vowel. The hunter pulled the front of his gun down and tapped the top of it with his free hand to empty the barrels of the shot gun so it could be reloaded. He reloaded with two cartridges and cocked the gun back up and swivelled round with lightning precision and let off another gunshot.

The pellets flew toward Foxy and as the cartridge blast broke in the air the pellets fragmented and one of them entered Foxy's shoulder, and another took off part of his left ear.

The hunter let out a celebratory cheer and pumped his fist into the increasingly greyer night. He ended his celebration by stomping his heavy workman boots into the damp mud and moved towards his prey.

Foxy was huddled in pain, his brain wanting to move but he could not. His body was saying, take a rest Foxy, you need it. This was no time for resting and Foxy extended his paw to move but his body would not allow it to any further. Nothing for it, Foxy stared at the hunter aware that this would be a horrible death and made the decision there and then not to beg and not to show fear.

"I could shoot you right now," said the hunter smiling, showing his tobacco stained teeth, "but first, first I want to have me some fun!"

The hunter let out an evil sadistic laugh as a smile went from ear to ear. He raised his shotgun high over his shoulder and wrapped it around his back. The hunter pulled his white sleeves, coated in blood, up to his elbows and pulled his bomber jacket down straight.

"This is gonna hurt you a lot more than it does me, that much is true," said the hunter and proceeded to pound on foxy with his dirty boots. Foxy was defenceless, this was a terrifying situation incomparable to anything Foxy had ever been through. The pain was immense and a far cry from the so called boxing match with Dino. The hunter laid a few more blows on Foxy.

"Stupid fox," laughed the hunter. "This land is ours. Ours you hear. What're you gonna do about it eh?" The hunter raised his dirty boot on his right leg ready for the death stomp and let out a spine tingling evil, sadistic laugh.

For a moment Foxy nearly blacked out from the shock. He wondered if he was dead due to a red mist that had appeared before his eyes. This isn't my blood what on earth could it be? Foxy thought. Foxy slipped into unconsciousness.

There was a huge roar and a flash of orange light. The noise and light were not the sound of a gun or even a blast from a gun. It was Tiger. Tiger had jumped from high up and came crashing down on the hunter just as he was about to deliver the death blow to Foxy. The flash of light of her orange coat and the noise of her death inducing roar would strike fear into any man. Tiger lay on top of the hunter and in one striking motion, bit into him and ripped out his throat. The hunter's scream was only temporary and terminated once he died from Tiger's bite.

"Go report this to The Elders now!" Tiger ordered two fellow tigers that had accompanied her. The two tigers, obviously subordinates, turned and ran off back toward Tiger's habitat of heat and humidity down the long narrow path to the clearing.

Tiger walked calmly over to Foxy who was beginning to come around from his beating at the hands of the hunter.

"Foxy?" Tiger asked as Foxy began to stir a bit, his eyes partially open.

"What happened?" Foxy asked.

"You were attacked by a hunter."

"How bad is it?

"You will heal up," Tiger assured him. "You're suffering more from shock than anything else, I'd say," she said in a comforting way as Dino, clutching his arm, and Donkey came running towards Foxy and Tiger. Tiger looked at Dino, "You alright?" Tiger asked.

"Just a scratch," he replied. "How is he?" Dino asked.

"He'll live." Foxy got up and stood wobbly but proudly on his hind paws.

"What were they doing out here?" Tiger asked.

"They've come to take over The Jungle," Foxy replied, as Tiger looked on in disbelief. "They are moving in I tell you," Foxy parted his hands wide.

"Then the situation is graver than I thought, much graver indeed," Tiger said. High in the air was Crow who circled a few times in the grey air and dive-bombed down at a frenetic pace to land neatly on Tiger's shoulder. "This is Crow," said Tiger.

"Nice to meet you Crow," Foxy said. Foxy smiled at Crow but Crow said nothing back. Crow is the only animal in The Jungle that cannot speak. He squawks and the intonation of his squawks is something only Tiger can understand.

"SQUARRRRK!" Crow replied.

"Crow is my right hand bird. He looks out for danger high up in the skies. He spotted you being ambushed from way up in the sky."

"Amazing!"

"Crow, fly ahead and see if there are any more of this vermin out there!"

"SQUAAAARK!" Crow nodded and soared high into the air.

"He will find them," assured Tiger.

"With one eye?" Foxy asked.

"He only needs one. He lost his eye when he was a youngling. You will not find a better surveillance expert in the whole jungle. You didn't see the hunters with two eyes and heightened senses now did you?" Tiger said. Foxy looked at her, she's right he thought.

"Fair enough," conceded Foxy.

"Let's rest. Tell me what you know?" Tiger asked.

"Only that I..." Foxy fainted before finishing his sentence. Dino and Donkey looked concerned and moved in. Two more subordinate tigers appeared and approached Tiger instantly.

"Take him inside my cave," ordered Tiger to the two subordinate tigers. "Make sure that he gets rest." The two tigers nodded in synchronisation and moved towards Foxy. The first tiger grabbed Foxy by the head using his mouth while the other tiger did the same on Foxy's rear paws. They ran back off down the narrow path towards the clearing and Tiger's home.

8 - JUST WHAT DOES A TIGER'S CAVE LOOK LIKE ANYWAY?

The grey skies had darkened to form a more even black night. Tiger's cave was situated in the clearing deep within The Jungle territory. It was located away from the rest of The Jungle animals. It was a sign of respect for The Queen Of The Deep Jungle to have her own cordoned off area.

The cave was a stone, circular structure not dissimilar to an igloo minus the extreme cold and narrow entrance. There were two cut-outs in the cave, one for Tiger to enter through the front, and one a smaller hole high on the back of it, like a window for Tiger to gaze out into the beautiful starlit skies. The entire structure was about ten feet in height and eight feet in width. The front door hole was covered in a skin material from a hunt that acted as a door cover.

Inside Tiger's cave there was a large marble slab about six feet by two feet and cold to the touch. Tiger would sleep and stretch here after a long day. To the left of the cave lay some ornaments from hunts, trophies of a skull of a boar, spine of what looked ape in origin and an empty space. Tiger would probably fill that empty space with the skull of the hunter she had recently torn apart to save Foxy.

Foxy was lying on the right of the cave on a makeshift bed, an uneven slab of stone that would make you fall off if you were to move too much. Foxy was recovering and had a bandage made of a rag over his torn ear that had a few spots of blood on it. He had a sling on his arm made from a similar material to Tiger's cave entrance and a doc leaf over his right eye acting as a plaster to stop any bleeding.

Foxy had been out like a light for a few hours now, physically and mentally exhausted. The rest was doing him the world of good, and he had not been so sound asleep and safe in years. However, the trauma from earlier was still very much with him. When Foxy would fall asleep he would instantly feel better but when he awoke the painful memories of the day would come crashing back to haunt him.

Tiger strolled into her cave quietly but enough to make Foxy's eye peer over. Foxy jumped up.

"Relax," Tiger said as Foxy rubbed his paw on his head gently.

"How long was I out?" Foxy asked with a hint of pain in his voice.

"A couple of hours."

"I must get up," Foxy said throwing his legs around and planting his paws on the cold, comfortable mud surface floor. Tiger looked back at him.

"Rest," she ordered.

"No!" Foxy exclaimed.

Tiger looked back at Foxy unimpressed with his insubordinate tone; she was not used to someone questioning her. In The Deep Jungle she was Queen, ruler, soldier and leader with influence over everyone including The Elders of The Jungle. In her own cave, Tiger was even more supreme; this was her 'turf' and no one tells her what to do. Foxy had realised his mistake but he was not an invalid. He was a proud fox and he would not be treated as a weakling devoid of any dignity.

"Sorry," Foxy offered. Tiger moved to a more pressing matter.

"Crow came back from his surveillance," she said.

"And?"

"Not good," she said. "He flew all the way out to The Outer Territory where you came from. Beyond that he saw a massive complex, machine-like, populated by humans. The Conglomerate he called it."

"The Conglomerate?" Foxy was intrigued and wanting to know more.

"Yes. They will move further and further into The Jungle bit by bit before they take over the whole area and then what's stopping them doing this to the rest of The Jungle?"

"Yesh. The rest of the Continent could be next you know."

"The Continent!" Tiger exclaimed. "Who cares? All the rest of the Continent does is hunt my kind!"

"We must do something," Foxy said.

"I'm not sure we can," she said somewhat perplexed with it all.

"Listen," he replied and gently got up standing on his hind legs and paws. "We need to go there, do some extra surveillance. Surveillance from the ground, work on what Crow has already done."

"Go on."

"A scavenge operation."

"A scavenge operation?" Tiger said lacking no sarcasm in her dulcet tone.

"Yesh," he continued. "Stake the place out and then work on a plan to bring it down!" Foxy said with passion, passion that was clearly lost on Tiger. She lifted her head back and roared with laughter very deeply.

"Are you seriously suggesting that you, you go in there?" Tiger asked.

"Yesh," he replied.

"Foxy, Foxy, cocky foxy, foolish Foxy," she said. "You are indeed brave but stupid it would seem. Brave and stupid," she turned around a bit. Foxy made a few confident steps but ended up stumbling. The noise made Tiger turn back, she offered a paw to help stabilise Foxy. Foxy slapped her paw away in defiance and disappointment.

"Damn it Tiger!" shouted Foxy. "I'm a scavenger. I'm built for this. You either get someone to go with me or I'll go on my own. What'll it be?" Foxy asked confidently. Tiger stared back at Foxy looking for a hint of weakness on his war battered face.

"I... I can't." Tiger replied.

"Can't or won't?"

"Look. It's too dangerous."

"Just give me a person, that is all I need, just one of your soldiers."

"I won't risk them."

"Fine." Foxy finished and hobbled towards the cave entrance to leave.

"Where are you going?"

"To stake out The Conglomerate and find vulnerability in there!"

"Wait!"

"What, you can't spare the tiger power you said!"

"No Foxy," said Tiger. "I said it's too dangerous for others. But not for Tiger," she said. A wry smile crept over Foxy's furry face, but ceased when the creases from his face muscles hurt him.

"You mean it?" Foxy asked.

"How do you say it? Yesh." Tiger said playfully mocking Foxy's way of saying 'affirmative'.

"Yesh!" Foxy gleefully replied.

"I'm coming with you then. And Crow is coming too. He could be useful."

"Great let's go!" Foxy said. Tiger nodded in agreement and Tiger exited the cave with Foxy not far behind her.

9 - THE SURVEILLANCE MISSION AND STAKE OUT WITH AN EXPLANATION OF FOXISMS

Foxy leant up against the exterior of Tiger's cave, brushed himself down and steadied himself. He was ready. Foxy took a glance over to Tiger, who was on all fours and looked strong as always. Tiger waited for a moment and in the distance a squawk noise could be heard with a faint black dotted spec seen on the horizon flying towards them with much grace and speed.

"SQUAAAAAWWWWWWWWWWWWWK," yelled Crow as he flew into view as if he was an aeroplane coming to land on a runway. Crow let his speed drop. Using his wings raised high, he fluttered them gently to control his descent and pointed them upwards. Crow's descent was as smooth as silk as he landed flawlessly on Tiger's right shoulder and fluttered his wings a final time before resting them on his back.

"Foxy need a ride?" Tiger asked offering her back to Foxy.

"Foxy care not for ride!" Foxy replied slightly insulted.

"Suit yourself," replied Tiger as she turned around, away from her cave and faced an audience of tigers. The tigers were Tiger's soldiers, loyal to her and The Elders. She walked in front and looked into the night air, counted the stars and looked back at her tiger soldiers. Tiger was proud of her soldiers, each of them were brave and stood as if they were ready to die for her should she command it. "Tigers!" Tiger said. "This is a two person operation..."

"SQUAAARRRKK!" Crow protested.

"Pardon me Crow," she said, "a three person operation," Tiger continued. "We are going over to The Conglomerate to find information and look for a vulnerability, any vulnerability or clue to help us in our ultimate goal to stop humans taking over our jungle. Any questions?"

"Ur what's a conglomerate?" Donkey asked, sat not too far back from the tigers with Dino next to him paying attention.

"Let me explain Tiger," Foxy butted in. "Now Donkey, imagine you had one Jim. Okay? Now this Jim decided that he wanted another Jim, but in another area doing something else? Okay? Now, you have more Jim's specialising in different areas. This is a conglomerate, a company that has many businesses in many different areas." Foxy was rather proud of himself and how he linked it to something even Donkey could understand. It made Foxy smile.

"But Jim bad, Foxy?" Donkey asked with his head down saddened.

"No Donkey it's just an example," Foxy said trying to calm Donkey.

"Jim!"

"Go on Tiger," Foxy said. Tiger scowled at Foxy as if to say 'this is my show fox, don't you push it now.'

"Don't push it Foxy," she said under her warm breath from the heat. "We will be back in a few hours. If we are not… then wait more." Tiger said looking at Foxy, very proud of her arrogant comment.

"Nice," replied Foxy.

"Roll out!" Tiger ordered and the entourage of tigers moved aside and parted like Moses and the Red Sea.

As Foxy and Tiger walked through them, Foxy caught Dino's gaze. Dino, once an enemy of Foxy who had given him a chiding in the ring not so long ago, was genuinely worried about his new found friend. Foxy also looked at Dino with a similar respect and new found friendship.

"Come back soon Foxy," Dino said.

"Hey, I will be back in two shakes of a fox's tail," Foxy confidently replied. Foxy and Tiger strolled off out of the clearing and onto their mission. Donkey and Dino stood there and watched Foxy and Tiger walk off into the distance. When Foxy and Tiger could no longer be seen Donkey and Dino stared at each other, turned and walked into the clearing.

A bit later, Foxy and Tiger strolled along with Crow on Tiger's right shoulder. Foxy was walking on his hind legs while Tiger was still on all fours. She was alert and ready for anything.

The area they were in now was less humid than Tiger's home, it was still dark and the stars had switched around in the sky as the trio walked in a new direction. There were trees of a great height all around and a path was clearly formed on the ground from having been trodden on many times. Foxy, Tiger and Crow followed the downtrodden path. Sometimes Foxy stood on all fours to try and pick up a scent of a hunter, other times he reverted back to his hind legs and changed the direction of his walking. It was then that Foxy decided to break the awkward silence with some small talk with Tiger.

"What do you do for food, Tiger?" Foxy asked.

"Tiger eats good food," she replied clearly puzzled by the comment. "Why do you ask?"

"Because, look!" Foxy shouted and hurried along. "There's a chicken down there!" Foxy ran towards it on all fours. As Foxy approached the chicken, he salivated at the half eaten carcass. The carcass was not quite flea ridden or smelly, it looked like road kill with some meat and feathers on display. Foxy tucked right into the carcass creating noises that could not be interpreted.

"Ra rag u rah! Grr yug uk rug gah rag rag rah! Ra rag u rah!" Foxy said clearly hungry.

"Foxy!" Tiger shouted with a noticeable level of disgust. "What're you doing? That... that thing! It could be disease ridden!" Tiger said.

"Squawk," agreed Crow. Foxy tilted his head towards Tiger and looked at her with his orange and green marble coloured eyes. Foxy had some feathers coming out of his mouth.

"But, I was hungry!" Foxy said innocently. Tiger stared at Foxy momentarily speechless. "It's great Tiger... GULP. MUNCH, MUNCH! Care to try?" Foxy offered.

"No no no!" Tiger said with a paw raised in protest. "Tiger only eats fresh produce!"

"Each his own," proclaimed Foxy and turned back to the carcass.

"Come on Foxy. We need to reach there by sunset," interrupted Tiger. Foxy reluctantly got up and followed Tiger and they continued walking along the path.

"Look Tiger, smoke."

"Yes indeed."

"Then this path is right, it will lead us straight to The Conglomerate. Yesh," Foxy said, proud of his tracking skills. As they walked, the path started to meander a bit and began to arc around. The smoke was still visible in the distance of the night sky. As they went further down the path, the smell of sulphur from the smoke made it apparent that they could not be far from a large facility of some kind. Perhaps the smoke would emanate from a large chimney tower, Foxy thought.

"Round and round we go, where we end up, nobody know. Nobody know," Foxy joyfully said in verse.

"Foxy?" Tiger asked looking at Foxy.

"Yesh?"

"What... or where did you get these strange sayings from?"

"What do you mean?"

"I mean, 'yesh', 'round and round blah blah blah' and two shakes of a fox's tail etc?"

"Oh, those are Foxisms," Foxy proudly replied.

"Foxisms?" Tiger asked.

"Yesh."

"Right, and what is a foxism?"

"A foxism is a saying invented by me, Foxy to describe an event or a situation."

"Okaaaaay," said Tiger strangely.

"Yesh, round and round we go, where we end up nobody know,"

"Yes Foxy but what does it mean?"

"We go round and round and where do we end up?" Foxy asked Tiger.

"Uh," replied Tiger with a shrug of her shoulders, confused.

"Exactly!" Foxy replied, "nobody know, nobody know," he said.

"Right, ok," she replied.

They continued to walk along the path for some time before they could see The Conglomerate in the distance. It was a huge structure, ominous looking with a large chimney stack emitting smoke high up in the air that disrupted the beauty of The Jungle. It was a large steel building, box shaped with many floors and had a wire fence surrounding it. On top of the fence was some barbed wire, very sharp to keep out any intruders. There were video cameras on every wall and some hunters walking around the perimeter.

"Not much farther now," Foxy said.

"Darn, look at that," said Tiger staring ahead of their path, at a large mound about twenty feet in height and very wide. "We can go over it but The Conglomerate will see us. We can't go around we will lose time. Crow! Go and have a look in the air to see how exposed we will be."

"Squaaaaawwwwwwk," obeyed Crow.

"No Crow," said Foxy as Tiger looked at him curiously. "Let's go under!"

"Under? And, how do we do that Einstein?" Tiger mocked.

"Simple physics my dear Tiger. Spin my tail would you, Tiger?" Foxy asked.

"You what?" Tiger replied.

"My tail," he replied pointing his bottom in the air with his bushy tail on display.

"You want me to spin your tail?"
"Yesh."
"Why?"
"Tiger, spinning my tail creates Foxy Power. Once my tail starts it spins like a helicoptor," he said.
"A what?"
"Nevermind, foxism my Tiger."
"Grrrr," Tiger replied.
"Pull it down," he ordered. Tiger approached his tail and stood on her hind legs. With her front legs, she grabbed hold of Foxy's tail and whipped it down. As she did Foxy's tail came to life spinning round quickly just like a helicopter with a lot of speed. "Watch this!" Foxy said with excitement. "Diggin' Foxy Power! Foxy Power!"

Foxy took his front paws and clawed at the mound. With blistering speed he had dug right under the mound. Within seconds, Foxy had disappeared from view and could no longer be heard digging. Tiger looked at Crow somewhat impressed with her mouth open, but tried her best to disguise it.
"Where'd he go?" Tiger asked.
"Squaawwwwwwk," shrugged Crow.
"Strange," said Tiger.

Suddenly, Foxy's head appeared out of the entrance hole that he had created and coughed up some mud.
"All done. Well don't just stand there, have you never seen a tunnel before? Let's go! Tiger's first?" Foxy said before getting out and motioning Tiger to enter the hole first. Tiger walked and tripped on a loose piece of mud and fell backwards. Foxy leapt forward and grabbed her to prevent her from falling painfully on her back.
"Whoa! Careful Tiger," Foxy said.
"Release me now!" She ordered.
"Okay, okay Tiger don't get excited!"

"Foxy, being held by you isn't quite enough to get me excited!" Tiger replied.

"Well sorry, Tiger," replied Foxy, "but we haven't got time for anything else." Foxy winked at Tiger, walked past her and entered the hole first himself.

"Grrrrrr," she replied huffing and puffing with anger at Foxy.

"Squaaawwwk Squaaaarrrrk," Crow said with a glitter of humour in his remaining eye.

Crawling through the tunnel Foxy had made was a struggle for Tiger with her larger frame of body. For one thing, Crow had to move from his position on her shoulder to under her arm/leg pit and Tiger was nigh on flat and pulling herself forward rather than crawling along.

"Next time Foxy, consider that others larger than a fox may use your tunnels," she said in frustration.

"Go on a diet," Foxy replied under his breath.

"I beg your pardon!" Tiger replied.

"Go on and try it," Foxy replied proud of getting away with his joke.

After five minutes of crawling through, Foxy could see the end of the tunnel and pulled himself out of it. Tiger followed, a bit dirtier and Crow emerged from under her leg. The Conglomerate was even closer now and they were a stone's throw away from the fences.

"There it is," Foxy said. It was a magnificent sight of industrialisation, large, intimidating, solid steel and looked impregnable. It was impossible to tell what was inside as there appeared to be no window, just solid steel, with video cameras at the top moving continuously to pick up any intruder on the move.

"It's huge," Tiger commented.

"Imagine, this taking over the whole jungle! I mean look at it, they are expanding at a rapid pace. Think what must've been here before this? They could take over the whole jungle," Foxy replied.

"Squaaaaaark," agreed Crow.

"Not in MY jungle," said Tiger.

"Squaaaaaark," crow again agreed.

"Foxy. What do you suggest?"

"Hmm, let Foxy think," he replied surveying the area with narrowed eyes. "Hmm, the barbed wire is too dangerous and covers everything but we must get in," Foxy said thinking aloud. "Also, we could tunnel in and create a long term plan of multiple tunnels for entry points for a surprise attack. No Foxy, that's no good, not enough time." Foxy looked to the far left of The Conglomerate through the barbed wire fence and spotted some large drums, two in total, filled with oil or a highly explosive fuel. When Foxy scanned to the far right of The Conglomerate he saw a further two oil drums. "Foxy know, where to go!"

"Cut the Foxism's Foxy what do you suggest?" Tiger said impatiently.

"Yesh. You see those drums?"

"What's a drum?"

"Those large cylinder things over there, see them?"

"Yes."

"They are full of oil. If you put a match in it or a spark to make fire, then bye bye banana don't get any on ya, Boooooooooom! All gone!" Foxy shouted.

"How do you know?"

"Tiger, I've been in places similar to this…" Foxy paused for a second, deep in thought. Foxy thought back to his many scrapes and adventures in the past. Sure, he had been to some bad places but nothing of this size, but the thought of fire made him pause. "Plus fire is something these hunters use to kill my cousins and drive us out of the forests and jungles."

"But why hunters?"

"I guess they work for The Conglomerate, whoever runs it to ensure there is no resistance to their expansion plans in The Jungle."

"Hmm, but we can't get in there."

"Not now. But perhaps in a group of force we could. We would have to have a whole army of animals to do it. Surely we can do that? We'd outnumber them! Still too dangerous?" Foxy appealed. Tiger, sat down on her hind legs and stretched out her front legs resting on her paws and then sat back and thought about it.

"Yes. The risk is very, very high. We don't know how many people, hunters or whoever are beyond those steel walls. But the risk is worth the reward. To do nothing means we are dead anyway," Tiger concluded.

"Yesh."

"Crow!" Tiger shouted.

"SQUAAAAARRRK?" Crow asked.

"Take a mental image of this beast of a structure. We will use it for schematics and devise a plan of attack for later. Go!" Tiger ordered.

"Squarrrrrrk!" Crow replied and flew high into the black night completely camouflaged with his tar black feathers against the night.

"You were right. He's good. Very good," said Foxy.

"Yes. When he's not sick," she replied.

"Sick?" Foxy asked.

"Yes, when I was a young cub I was out playing and saw something dark fall from the sky. I'd no idea what it was. I ran up to it curious of what it was. It was a crow with a broken wing, his eye was also missing back then," Tiger paused for a second and swallowed. "I nudged him with my nose and he squawked back at me. He made me smile. Funny how I didn't consider eating him really. Anyway, I picked him up in my mouth and took him to a secret hiding place. It was here we discovered how to communicate with each other. Somehow I understood that he wanted his wing set in a position like this." Tiger simulated moving her front leg into a recovery position. "Eventually his wing grew strong and it was time for him to fly away. He never did and as I grew older and stronger, Crow was older and wiser. I guess he feels he owes me his life. He never considers his health before helping Tiger." Tiger stopped and looked into the sky. Foxy looked back at Tiger enthralled by what he had just heard. After a few seconds Foxy looked up to the sky with Tiger.

"How long will it take?"

"Not long."

"Good. Because there are hunters over there on patrol, look."

"Darn."

"Take cover," Foxy said.

Along the perimeter of the box steel beast of The Conglomerate, there were four hunters moving along the side of the fence. When they got to the end of the fence, they would walk back again keeping the same pattern of movement. They were clearly in sight of Foxy and Tiger.

"What about Crow?" Foxy asked.

"Crow knows the risk. He will fly back to where we were. If we're not here he will just fly back home. He's been briefed earlier," Tiger said.

"Damn," Foxy replied.

"Let's move back to the tunnel," she said. As Foxy and Tiger turned around they stepped on something in the ground as lights from The Conglomerate lit up. The perimeter and outside the steel fence were now fully lit. Foxy and Tiger were completely visible under the harsh bright lights. The four hunters were alerted and the noise of sirens echoed out like something out of a World War II prison film.

"Darn! Crow, I hope you're on the move. And Foxy," Tiger said.

"Yesh?"

"Get your tail into gear!"

"Yesh. I'm on it."

As Foxy and Tiger ran back towards the entrance to the hole, a hunter appeared in front of them. Tiger and Foxy sprinted at a dizzying pace, but the hunter reacted by raising his double barrelled shot gun in their direction, closed one eye and aimed in preparation to fire.

"Tiger! Hunter direct ahead!" Foxy shouted.

"You mean food," replied Tiger.

Before the hunter could get off a shot, Tiger had jumped off with such force that she landed right on top of the hunter. The hunter looked petrified as he collapsed on the floor like a sack of potatoes. Tiger sunk her canines deep into the hunter's neck and pulled back with such force that it left the hunter limp like a piece of string.

Crow flew back into view from the sky and landed onto Tiger's shoulder.

"Crow! You disobeyed protocol! I told you always fly home in danger!" Tiger shouted.

"Squarrrrk!" Crow apologised.

"There are more coming. Here comes another, Tiger! I hope you're hungry!" Foxy proclaimed.

"Tiger skipped breakfast. It's feast time!" The second hunter stood in front of Foxy and Tiger. This time the hunter did not even have time to lift his shotgun as Tiger launched into him and sunk her teeth deep into his stomach. There were gunshots all around. On the ground where Tiger and Foxy ran, the mud flicked up due to the pellets and bullets hitting the ground around them with such force.

"There stop that tiger and fox!" A hunter, who had appeared about twelve metres in front of them, screamed. The entrance to the mound that Foxy had dug was only six meters away. They could make it.

Foxy leapt head first into the mound and Tiger followed with Crow back under her leg pit

"Down here Tiger, quick!" Foxy screamed. Tiger went down the hole shortly after Foxy and squeezed her way through the tight, narrow tunnel. Foxy had to slow his pace down, waiting for Tiger to catch up and they made it to the middle of the dark tunnel.

Meanwhile, outside, one of the hunters stood over the mound and pointed his gun down the entrance of the tunnel. Another hunter appeared from over the way and looked around.

"There! You! Get to the front of the mound and stop them from coming out! I will stay at this end in case they double back," the hunter shouted.

"Aye Sir!" The hunter cried back, turned sharply, gun in hand and sprinted across to the other side of the mound as fast as he could. There was no doubt that he would make it to the exit that Foxy and Tiger were heading for due to Tiger's lack of speed and space in the tunnel. It was not looking good.

Inside the mound, the tunnel was dark and damp. Foxy, Tiger and Crow were near the exit and felt relieved at the thought of getting out of the mound.

"Come on quick!" Foxy called, with excitement. Foxy charged forward and his head was near the exit of the tunnel when it hit something, not hard luckily, but enough to make him stop. Foxy paused and took a step back to gather his thoughts. What have I run into? Foxy thought. Foxy took a closer look and noticed that the long object, obscured by darkness was moving very smoothly left and right and looked like two pipes. It was clear to Foxy what this was, a hunter's gun.

"Update Foxy?" Tiger asked.

"Back up, Back up!" Foxy shouted.

"Why?" Tiger asked unable to see past Foxy.

"Hunter and gun this end," replied Foxy.

"Darn! Back to the entrance quickly." Tiger was unable to turn around due to the narrowness of the tunnel, so she had to crawl backwards.

"Tiger, I'm going to dig under you a bit and make this a bit wider. This way you will have a little bit more room in this part of the tunnel. Also I can run ahead and see if the entrance is clear," Foxy said.

"Good idea Foxy," Tiger replied. Foxy started to dig with his paws, but without the aid of his tail to propel him he was a bit slower than before, but still he dug, and he dug deep. As he dug under Tiger, she was able to move her legs a bit and get more space and felt less squashed. Foxy emerged after having got past Tiger and hurried off to the entrance. Foxy reached the entrance and did not need to examine what was waiting for him at this end. Just like at the other end, there was the familiar barrel of the shotgun pointing down. Foxy turned and hot tailed it back to the middle of the tunnel where Tiger lay.

"Now what?" Tiger asked seeing Foxy running back towards her.

"Stay here in the middle," Foxy replied.

"Why?" Tiger asked.

"Hunter, other side too."

"We're trapped!" Tiger panicked.

"Relax," he said.

"I can't!" Tiger replied.

"Why? What do you mean you can't? What's up?" Foxy asked.

"I don't like tight concealed spaces!" This admission surprised Foxy. How on earth could The Queen Of The Jungle be afraid of tight spaces? She was all powerful and made no complaint of the journey through the tunnel? I guess she must be hiding her fear, Foxy thought. Foxy was unable to hide his curiosity even in a moment of impending death such as this.

"You live in cave! How can you be scared of tight concealed spaces?" Foxy asked.

"A cave Foxy," she said, "not a mud hole you foolish fox."

"I've lived in worse than this!"

"Do something!" Tiger ordered.

"Okay, okay alright hang on. Just don't panic, dang it. Let me think." Foxy went quiet and started to think. Tiger looked at his brow and saw his mind was working overtime. Foxy was thinking, thinking of every impossible situation he had ever faced in his life and how he got out of it. He always found a way, how would this be any different? It wouldn't, he would always find a way out. Foxy clicked the stubby digits on his paw together, not dissimilarly to how a human clicks their fingers, as if a magic idea had arrived. His idea was halted and put aside when the hunters outside fell quiet.

"Maybe they went?" Tiger said in the cold, quiet eerie tunnel.

"Doesn't make sense," said Foxy. He was right, after all they were trapped. The hunters could've stayed there all day. The only seemingly plausible option to get out of there would be for Foxy to dig with Tiger there, although it would have been possible, it would have been extremely slow. The hunters could just wait all day for their prey to come out of the hole and shoot.

Foxy started to sniff. He sniffed a few times to the left and to the right. His eyes widened with terror and Tiger noticed his concern.

"What?" Tiger asked.

"No!" Foxy said.

"What?"

"Nothing."

"Foxy tell me what is wrong?" Tiger ordered and Foxy sniffed into the air again, a smell of wood with a hint of oil, he had smelt this before.

"Smoke. They're burning us out. It's worse. I smell oil too. Fire, it's getting closer!" A sheer look of terror passed over Tiger.

"We'll be burnt alive. Help!" Tiger screamed. Foxy had been in jams many times before and had learnt never to panic even with a situation as severe as this, but even he had to admit to himself that this was a horrible situation. In truth, Foxy was unable to think what to do, he had been responsible for getting them into this and he would have to be responsible for getting them out.

"Relax Tiger," was the only comfort Foxy could give. He glanced to the left then right, sniffed and determined that the fire was closing in quicker from the right but he could not gamble on there being no fire to the left. The choice was simple, up or down. Foxy concluded that up would take them out clearer but with death inevitable from a gunshot. So Foxy was left with going down, but the flames would still follow them, it was simple physics. Fire would burn as far as there was oxygen, Foxy thought. Foxy realised he would have to gamble on something though. The gamble would have to be that he could dig quicker than the fire could burn, according to the law of physics of course. Damn what has happened to you fox? Foxy thought to himself, and slapped himself around the face to get him out of the mess of his thoughts. Foxy had decided enough was enough.

"Foxy?" Tiger asked, concerned that he was thinking too much.

"Okay," Foxy said in confidence ready to deliver a plan to the panicked Tiger. "Two choices. We go up or down," Foxy said.

"Up?" Tiger replied.

"No, no, no. Not good. They could shoot us as soon as we break free from the mound. Actually," said Foxy, "you know, let's go down and then up. There's not enough room to propel my tail so it will take me a bit longer to pick up enough speed to dig through. But I'll be back." Foxy dug very quickly, within seconds he was submerged under the damp, dark and cool mud.

"Foxy come back!" Tiger screamed.

Foxy's head momentarily emerged from the mound, covered in mud.

"Tiger! I'll be back. You saved my life once. I won't forget it. I'm coming back, you hear me?" Foxy said and Tiger, clearly frightened nodded back. Foxy then looked towards Crow, "Crow, keep her calm buddy and keep an eye on her, no pun intended," Foxy said.

"SQUAAAAAARKKK!" Crow agreed.

Foxy commenced digging leaving only Tiger and Crow alone to face the fire.

"Foxy!" Tiger shouted. It was no use, Foxy was not even close to hear her cries. To the left of Tiger, fire and smoke had closed in quickly and the fire to the right was coming in even quicker. Tiger was unable to move forward because if she did her only escape, down, would be blocked by fire. Maybe I should take my chances and go left? Tiger thought. And where on earth was Foxy? Had Foxy been caught or shot or worse burnt to death? Tiger stopped thinking and closed her mind off to the horrible images of her subconscious and decided to close her eyes. She pushed Crow deep into her arm/leg pit and protected him. She knew that there was a good chance that Crow would be safe while Tiger burnt to death.

The fire was now about an inch away from Tiger. This was it, nothing to do now, time to die.

Suddenly, Foxy crashed out of the newly dug hole covered in mud and panted and gasped for breath desperately.

"Foxy!" Tiger cried.

"Okay, Okay," coughed Foxy repeatedly. "We're clear, I found a way out of here. We have to go now. Tiger go first and crawl quick like you've never crawled before. The space is bigger than I normally dig. Now go, now," Foxy replied pushing Tiger down.

"But Foxy there's little room for both of us," she stated.

"Then stop discussing it and let's get a move on. Go now!" Foxy ordered.

Tiger crawled down as far as she could. Foxy started running behind her with the fire closing in on him. Tiger was indeed moving quickly, quicker than earlier. But, Foxy was losing his fight against physics. The oxygen in the tunnel was being kind to the fire and was right on top of Foxy and he felt his tail get extremely warm. He had time to look over his shoulder in fear of his thick bushy tail catching fire. His fears were confirmed when he saw the tail catch alight. It could only have been a single spark of flame that set the tail alight but his whole tail was engulfed like a Guy Fawkes figure on firework night. Foxy let out a whimper of pain as his hair on his tail had burnt off and the flesh was now being cooked.

"What's that light?" Tiger asked as she looked back towards the light.

"Stop looking back, keep going. Faster. We are almost there!" Foxy cried out in pain.

"Ok Foxy," she replied. They were indeed almost free and Tiger could smell the fresh air from the new tunnel that Foxy had dug. He must have dug his little heart out, she thought.

Within seconds she was clear. Crow came out from under her arm/leg pit and perched himself back on her shoulder. They were now quite a way from The Conglomerate; Tiger could not even see it in the distance. There were trees everywhere and they were in a deep forest in The Jungle. Even she was not sure where they were. There was no time for this now, she thought, Crow could get them home. But what of Foxy?

"Where's Foxy?" Tiger cried.

"Squaaarrrkkk!" Crow said unsure. "Squaaaaaaaaaaaaaaaarrrrkkkkkkkkk!" Crow alerted as loud as he could. A fireball came crashing out of the hole. It was Foxy, completely engulfed in flames, his tale was ashes.

"Darn. Foxy don't move," she ordered and leapt on Foxy with all her weight and flattened him like a pancake. It worked, the fire was extinguished. Tiger got up slowly off of Foxy, not sure if she had saved his life or flattened him to death. She looked at foxy and pushed him with her head rather gently. Nothing. She then licked his face causing Foxy to stir. His fur was surprisingly intact, except for his tail which was now just bone. It looked painful.

"Squaaarrrrrk?" Crow asked.

"No. He's not. He's still alive," she replied.

"Squarrrk," Crow said relieved.

"Help him onto my back Crow."

"SQUAWWWK!"

Crow flew off of Tiger's shoulder and glided smoothly onto the mud by Foxy's tail. Crow shook his head in disbelief at the condition of Foxy. As Crow surveyed Foxy, Tiger moved into position by Foxy's head. She stared and bent her head down by the back of Foxy's neck. Gently, she opened her jaws and bit into Foxy's flap of skin on his neck for grip and propelled her head backward sharply to toss Foxy in the air. At the other end of Foxy, Crow did the same but had his beak around Foxy's sharp, bony tail. The momentum of the swing sent Foxy high in the air and he performed a three hundred and sixty degree flip that had him land cleanly on Tiger's back.

"Is he secure?" Tiger asked Crow.

"Squarrrk!" Crow confirmed.

"Let's go Crow."

"Squark!" Crow agreed. Tiger made one final check that Foxy was secure and started to walk deeper into The Jungle.

The night sky was now growing lighter and it would not be long before dawn would appear. The night air was cool and quite calm in this part of The Jungle. Tiger took in her surroundings and was enamoured of the beauty of the environment. Tiger thought it a shame that soon, if The Conglomerate got their way, this would all be destroyed and turned into a steel beast like the abomination of a building they had just witnessed. Tiger walked slowly with Crow on her shoulder taking a moment before ordering Crow high into the air to find them a way back to The Deep Jungle of Tiger's home.

10 – THE CONGLOMERATE

The Conglomerate was a vast and impressive piece of modern day architecture, floor upon floor of steel industrialisation and commercialism rolled into one. The opening to The Conglomerate was a double wooden door, about ten feet wide with steel around the edges of it and protruding metal spikes. Beyond the doors lay the lobby to the heart of The Conglomerate. At night it was empty except for some human security guards keeping watch. The lobby was open plan with a receptionist desk as soon as you enter and room for six people to sit to man the phones. In front of the reception area were some chairs for 'guests' to sit. On the wall to the left of the lobby was a huge television screen, currently turned off. Past the lobby entrance was a huge spiral staircase that meandered up to the level above.

The next level of The Conglomerate was a vast array of offices similar to a modern day office setup. It had a corridor down the middle of the floor with each part of the corridor taking you to a section of the office. Each section was blocked off with glass to give the workers privacy. This was the ultimate corporate building where the drones could work on their electrical computer equipment and make The Conglomerate billions in revenue.

Each floor was remarkably similar with the exception of the top floor. The top floor was strictly off limits, even to the humans in a senior position in The Conglomerate. At the top of the spiral staircase was another wooden door the same size as the entrance to The Conglomerate, also with steel borders and metal spikes around the door. This door however had a retinal scanner to the right of it. Only the very important people of The Conglomerate were allowed in here, no one else.

On this evening, the door was shut, no one was inside and no one was outside. However, the room would soon become occupied.

The floor on this highest level revealed a sticky residue that shone under the harsh office lights. The sticky substance was reminiscent of what a slug may leave in its trail as it walks, or should that be slithers along? The stairs began to shake, something was walking up them. The noise took the form of a 'boom, pause, boom, boom and pause'. Something big was walking up the stairs, something struggling for breath.

A huge figure obscured in a cloak walked up the stairs and arrived at the top. As the figure walked towards the door, the sticky substance became evident. It was a trail this 'thing' left in its wake. The figure wore a long, scarlet coloured robe and on its head a hood obstructing the facial features. The figure must have been seven foot, maybe eight. It walked with a slow rhythm and a heartbeat to match. It moved over to the retinal scan machine, let out a sigh and leant forward. The figure had not quite leant forward enough to get a scan, so it moved its arms up to the hood of the robe and pulled it back just a touch but not enough to reveal its face. Its hands though were an odd colour, not quite flesh coloured and not quite green in colour but somewhere in-between. The figure leant forward and again let out a sigh.

"Access granted," the machine spoke. "Welcome Gore, good evening," the machine continued. Suddenly the wooden door made a huge noise of internal locks unbolting and it opened inward with a huge creaking sound. A flash of light came out through the doors as Gore walked through and pulled his hood back up.

Gore walked forward. In his room was a desk at the far end of the office. To the sides were shelves full of books stacked high to the ceiling and a doorway on each side leading off to further, smaller rooms. Gore walked towards the desk leaving a horrible snail trail behind him. What on earth was this substance? Gore approached the desk and the lights lit the office. Gore remained covered in his robe, head to toe.

Gore stopped, lifted his arms up to his hood and whipped it back to reveal a large dome of a head with sparse hair on top, black in colour with some greying. From this angle he appeared human. He stopped. Then a juddering of his shoulders started but with no noise, then the juddering got faster and more obvious, followed by a noise. This continued for about thirty seconds. Gore was laughing, and laughing hard, very hard. The noise was loud, incredibly loud.

"MUHAA HAH HAH HA HAH," laughed Gore. Suddenly he whipped his head around to reveal his face. His face was one only a mother could love; correction, not even a mother could love this face. He had bulbous eyes and an even more bulbous nose and looked very frog like. In fact, he looked like a cross between a human and a frog. There was clearly some kind of genetic defect or even a mutation. The laughing was unreal.

To the right out of one of the rooms appeared another human. Only this human looked like a human, short, obese, wearing wireframe glasses with a permanent frown on his face as if he were in agony. He walked toward Gore with more of a waddle than a confident walk.

"HAHAHAH, Cough cough," Gore said, in pain no doubt from the laughter as the other human waddled up closer to him.

"Sir," the tubby human said.

"Speak Toad!" Gore replied. Toad, was the name for the short obese human. Toad leant his head back and made a noise in his throat to bring up excess phlegm in his airways. Once he had done this he proceeded to spit it all over the floor. Well, it was not as if anyone would notice now was it? Especially not with all the discharge made from Gore.

"Sire, I hear the spies were taken care of," said Toad with a clearer voice.

"Where are they?" Gore shouted.

"It appears..." Toad paused, "that, in our anger they got away," he continued.

"Grrrrr..... COUGH COUGH!" Gore shouted in frustration. Gore's voice was the most boring voice in the world and it sounded like he should permanently be sucking cough sweets to give it some colour. "NO GOOD TOAD!" Gore screamed slamming his fist down on the desk before lifting his fist and opening his hand. As Gore opened his hand there was some webbing between the fingers, just like a frog. "I want them here," he continued. Go and get them!" Gore ordered.

"Sir," said Toad, "with respect they got away. What next?" Toad pleaded. Gore fired a look of disgust Toad's way.

"Toad, you are my second in command. Why are you asking me what next? You must devise a plan. I want these animals punished! The Conglomerate must take over and put a stranglehold on these animals! I want their homes! You hear me?" Gore shouted. Toad nodded in agreement but Gore was not finished. "Look at me," Gore said as he pointed to his head with his hands spread revealing the webbing between his fingers. "When I started steering The Conglomerate I had it in my head that this was the best way to expand. You get land. We own this land and we cut it down. Getting this far has made me… different. But it is this difference that makes me go one step further than anyone else and I will not stop until all my enemies are crushed. You must come up with a plan and clear this jungle. I've done it in the past and paid dearly. The toxic chemicals I used to destroy the parts of this jungle had complications and transformed me into what I am now. This is how far I'm willing to go. How far are you willing to go, Toad?" Gore asked with his hands still held up.

"Sir, I'm with you I always will be, but are you suggesting I use toxic chemicals? That would endanger all our workforce?" Toad replied.

"The Conglomerate must take over. I said you must do what is necessary. If the chemicals are the only way then so be it," Gore said.

"Sir. With respect. I'd like some help on this before I resort to a chemical attack."

"As you wish Toad, tell me what is the plan and who do you wish to recruit?" Gore asked.

"I was thinking master and I do have someone very special," Toad said excitedly. Gore looked at him as a smirk covered his big fat head.

"Good. Bring the man in," Gore ordered.

"Sir," replied Toad, looking very nervous indeed. Gore looked at Toad.

"Speak Toad!" Gore ordered. As he finished, Toad looked into the air and coughed up some excess phlegm and again spat on the floor.

"Well Master. It's not a he, well it may be, actually it is but…"

"Spit it out Toad!" Gore ordered. Toad misinterpreted the meaning of Gore's request and once again spat out some excess phlegm. Toad paused and realised what Gore actually meant.

"Oh right. Master it's an animal," Toad said, taking a step back.

"An animal!" Gore screamed. "The Conglomerate must have NO animals Toad!"

"But you Sir?" Toad answered. This angered Gore somewhat and the decibel level in his voice drastically increased.

"How dare you Toad? I am merely a frog lookalike due to the mutation of the chemical waste I used to get The Conglomerate started! I was willing to go that extra mile, something you seem to be lacking! I am Conglomerate through and through. I am NOT an animal. Do you know how hard it was for me to gain control over this land? No easy feat, let me tell you. The Conglomerate was human exclusive and looking the way I did took all of my ruthlessness and cunning to carve an effective Conglomerate. I want those animals dead! I hate them! Kill them Toad."

"I will obey, my master. But, please meet this recruit. It's all I ask. He's loyal without question," Toad said. "He gives his life to The Conglomerate. He's the kind of employee that never leaves work before his manager," added Toad.

"Oh, that is good, and?" Gore asked.

"He stays after work and can be seen working on critical projects even though there may be no obvious work," said Toad.

"Yes, yes, go on," Gore said.

"He'll always attend office functions and make all the conversations. He's the kind of employee that'll hold an umbrella over your head and get wet himself," Toad proudly said.

"Oh useful," Gore said his eyes widening.

"Yes, he will encourage a competitive environment in the workplace and do his utmost to secure his future progression in The Conglomerate, for the good of the corporation!" Toad cried.

"Oh!" Gore exclaimed.

"He'll use marketing terms that we all understand such as target, Blue Sky Thinking, proactive, burn rate and customer-centric so we can all nod in unison!" Toad added.

"Good," replied Gore.

"He's an expert at delegating work to others. Once they do the work he'll follow the correct procedures to lead it up the chain of command," Toad said proudly.

"Oh!" Gore said with smile.

"At least speak with him and I'm sure you'll find him a valuable asset." Toad pleaded, as Gore stroked his fat chin. Gore stopped and proceeded to stroke the fat under his main chin before opening his mouth. In what seemed like an eternity some noise came out of his mouth.

"So be it. Bring him in. But, remember this. No more animals Toad. I mean it," Gore ordered as Toad bowed to his master and took some steps backwards. Toad turned and went out of the room to the left.

Gore sat behind the desk and clicked his fingers loudly. From the right of the room, came another human with a trolley of two shelves crammed full of foods that made Henry VIII's dinners look like snacks. There were whole chickens, turkeys, pigs, boars and some vegetables. There was so much food that the human wheeling it along was cringing in pain. Eventually, he managed to get it to the side of Gore's desk. As he left, he bowed three times whilst walking backwards before leaving just as Toad had done. Gore began to tuck into his feast. A disgusting sight as he swallowed a chicken leg whole, sometimes he would just lift a plate up and let the contents slide off and go straight down his throat into his belly.

"I hate animals!" Gore muttered whilst chewing on a pigs hoof.

Toad entered leading his new companion into the room. It was a rat. The rat was about one foot in height and walked on its back legs upright with a very camp walk indeed. He was dark brown in colour and with every step he took he appeared more effeminate than before. The rat walked with his long, pink and thin tail trailing behind him. The sight of the rat walking in such an unmanly way, in Gore's eyes, made Gore suspicious and he kept his eyes fixed on the rat.

"Speak rat!" Gore shouted. The rat had a sickly smile on his face and his nose was brown, probably from trying to please his superiors too much. "What brings you here? You're an animal! Speak!" Gore roared.

"Hi master," said Rat with his upper arms extended flexing his tiny paws. "Well, I started off as an intern in The Conglomerate. You see, through general excelling, making my superiors happy, sacrificing my free time and delegation of tasks to hard working humans... I managed to get myself a key role as..."

"YARRGGGH. Boring rat!" Gore cried. "Why have you forsaken your own? You have one minute to convince me not to eat you!" Gore let out a roar. Rat, in a calm way, gulped and thought for a second.

"Okay," said Rat.

"Thirty seconds now Rat!" Gore said even though it had not been thirty seconds.

"Well... I was never accepted as a rat. I was the lowest of the low. Even foxes hate me," Rat said.

"GRRRR, I hate foxes," cried Gore.

"Me too master. So I got a successful career going in The Conglomerate. I'm never going back to that jungle. I want to serve my whole life to The Conglomerate and adopt the culture to my lifestyle and adapt to the corporate ways. Just the way my mentor Toad did! This is the way to be! In fact, if I had anything else in my life, I'd die! I know The Conglomerate. That is my life. I'd step on my own mother just to get a foothold higher in The Conglomerate. And if anyone is smarter than me, I'll use their talents as teamwork master to progress myself. I give myself to The Conglomerate. I am Conglomerate through and through," finished Rat. There was silence from Gore. He leant back in his chair and let out a huge sigh. Then, his shoulders started to move bit by bit and the deep noise of laughter came back up. Within seconds Gore was laughing uncontrollably and his shoulders moving at a blistering pace.

"Five seconds remaining. Rat with such efficiency while actually having done nothing, you truly deserve a place in The Conglomerate," said Gore. Gore then turned to Toad and shouted.

"Toad! Tomorrow The Conglomerate will move forward into The Deep Jungle. We take it down!"

"Yes my Master," replied Toad. "I will work on it with Rat."

"Do not fail me Toad," Gore ordered. "And Rat, Welcome."

11 – REFUGE IN THE DEEP JUNGLE

The surveillance mission had not gone quite according to plan and Foxy was once again healing in Tiger's cave, this time from burns.

Outside Tiger's cave, Tiger stood somewhat dejected. She was looking weather worn. She composed herself and looked out at the crowd that had assembled in front of her. She had spoken to The Elders of The Deep Jungle already, and they had decided what the occupiers of The Deep Jungle should do. While Tiger was the leader of The Deep Jungle, The Elders took all the important decisions. Among the crowd were Foxy's friends Donkey and Dino, who stood prominently among the tigers, leopards, pumas, apes and snakes of The Deep Jungle.

Tiger inhaled deeply and then exhaled even harder. She looked into the cool night air and noticed how beautiful The Deep Jungle was. Tiger thought back to her life in this beautiful jungle. She thought about how she grew up here, how proud she was that she had made The Deep Jungle so safe and for years there was no trouble from humankind. How could I have been so naive? Tiger thought, she thought about how she, the other animals and even The Elders had grown complacent. The habitants of this part of The Jungle all knew of humankind creating problems elsewhere but assumed they were untouchable. How wrong they were. Tiger almost laughed when she realised it took a small, cocky fox to knock some sense into her. As Tiger wrestled with her thoughts, it made her angry and she was full of regret. As she stared into the beautiful night, it made it even harder for her to address the animals knowing what they must do.

"Everyone," Tiger roared, "The surveillance mission is over. When we got to The Conglomerate, we were met with resistance. Foxy almost sacrificed himself for your Queen. We should be proud of him," she said. They were proud, especially Dino and Donkey. "However, The Conglomerate was powerful. They had human hunters everywhere, attacking us with weapons and fire," the mention of fire made Tiger scrunch her eyes shut. She shook her head hard. "When we arrived, we surveyed the area and discovered some oil drums, full of explosive materials. We devised a plan to take it down by exploding these oil drums. I ask you now for your opinion. Speak now, or be quiet forever." There was silence in the crowd. All of the animals looked at each other afraid to make the first move. "Look," she continued, "before I make a decision it's important I have your feedback." Tiger said, deep down knowing that this was all futile. The Elders had already told her they must pack up and move farther back, abandon their home. Someone suggest we leave, it will take the burden off of me, Tiger thought.

"Tiger," Dino opened his mouth, "I'm with you, we all are… but, consider this… we have our lives. Foxy, well Foxy almost lost his. I say enough's enough," Dino said looking at Donkey. Despite Donkey's nervousness, he was fully aware of what his decision could do to the mission, to his life and to Jill and Jim his lost family.

"Donkey go with Foxy and Tiger," said Donkey with false bravado.

"Not this time Donkey," Tiger replied. "This decision must be yours to make alone." The nerves got the better of Donkey and his Tourette's reappeared.

"Jim!" Donkey cried. Tiger looked at him and nodded, his opinion was noted. She looked further into the crowd.

"Next!" Tiger shouted. The crowd in front of Tiger began to part as an animal moved forward to be heard. It was Leopard.

"Tiger. I'm forced to agree with Dino. The Conglomerate is, well are, animals!" Leopard said in an ironic tone calling the humans of The Conglomerate animals in the sense of barbaric. "This is madness. We never thought they could get this far into The Jungle. Yet, here they are. We must draw back and regroup. Fall back. Make a new home and live to fight another day," he said.

This was music to Tiger's ears, Tiger needed to hear this; it made the decision of The Elder's easier to give. The animals had spoken. She would not look so bad speaking the next course of action especially as within the crowd all the animals were mumbling under their breath in agreement.

Tiger looked into the night air again and felt a sensation in her stomach, and not a nice one. It was the feeling of nerves or butterflies. But Tiger was no coward, so why was she getting these feelings? Tiger realised why, she felt cheated by The Elders and wondered could she have fought more for the cause? What am I about to do? Tiger thought. She inhaled deeply and once again exhaled harder.

"Ok. I understand," she said with true regret. "Maybe you're right. We cannot fight. We must retreat. Ok. Leopard, filter the news through the ranks. We leave immediately." Leopard nodded and turned around and began to jog through the crowd. The rest of the animals turned around with heads held low. Morale was truly at an all-time low not just for them but for Tiger. Something just did not feel right.

Foxy appeared out of the entrance to Tiger's cave. Foxy looked terrible, beaten up with a crutch made out of twisty tree branches sitting under his arm/leg pit. Foxy's tail was bandaged up over the now bone of tail with the bandage undoing itself as it wanted. Foxy still had the cut eyebrow and bruised face. He had looked better, and he had a fire in his belly having heard what was going on as he lay in the cave. Foxy's mind was going a mile a minute. I can't believe what I've just heard, Foxy thought. The pain Foxy felt physically was nothing to the pain he was feeling inside; cheated, disappointed, dejected and possibly defeated.

The fire in his belly was growing in strength and was the kind of fire he could have used when he first addressed a public crowd.

"No!" Foxy shouted limping out on the crutches out in front of the remaining crowd, stopping them from walking away and retreating. "We must stay and fight!" Foxy said with true grit and determination. Tiger intervened and walked next to Foxy and placed a paw near him.

"No Foxy," she said bluntly.

"We can't give in!" Foxy shouted and swiped away her paw. Tiger looked at him and lowered her voice.

"It's over Foxy."

"No," cried Foxy.

"Yes!" Tiger shouted. Leopard was watching from the distance and paused unsure whether to stay or go. "Leopard, carry out my plans. Go now!" Leopard turned and moved.

"No!" Foxy screamed and inside him there was a rage building up like a kettle that was boiling. Everyone in their life, animal or human has the capacity to see red and totally lose it and this was Foxy's moment to see red. His whole body began to shake. The weak, withered, battle-worn frame of his was suddenly given a strength that was powered by adrenaline and it took him over like a new spirit. "NOOOOOOOOOOOOOOOOOOOOOOOOO!" Foxy screamed, turned and threw his crutch he was walking on at the wall of Tiger's cave. The crutch shattered instantly and fell into pieces by the cave's entrance. Foxy was now more powerful than ever and walked towards Tiger who was now one with the crowd. Foxy addressed Tiger but he could have been addressing all of them, schooling them on the errors of their ways. "They invade our homes and we fall back. They take over entire parts of our jungle and we fall back. How many more times must we fall back? Well, I say no more! The line must be draw here. This far and no further! And I... I... Am going to make them pay for what they have done!" Foxy's eyes were glowing with power.

"Foxy, we are outmanned and outgunned," Tiger said signalling Leopard to continue.

"You, you believe that?" Foxy said staring at Tiger. Tiger said nothing. "What about the rest of you?" Foxy asked the gathered crowd. "Well? Are you happy to give up your homes? Move somewhere else, only for them to come and push us out again?" Foxy looked in the crowd, no animal could look him in the eye. "Well I for one ain't! You know how many times I've lost my home to these humans? Too many let me tell you. I won't let this happen again!" Foxy looked back at Tiger.

"I can't..." Tiger whispered.

"I'm sorry Tiger I didn't hear?" Foxy mocked.

"You don't understand," she replied.

"Oh I understand. The Elders pull the strings round here. I'm afraid you're nothing more than a puppet!" Foxy exclaimed.

"How dare you!" Tiger roared, and swiped at Foxy's face. It was a minor blow, but enough to move Foxy back. Tiger did not mean to hurt Foxy, she would have hit herself if she could, she was just frustrated. Foxy stood up, tall and proud, looked into the crowd and walked towards the cave. The crowd looked at Tiger at first unsure what to do, then lowered their heads. Tiger felt miserable as if she had let herself down. What of The Elders? Tiger thought. Tiger felt sick at the thought of being a puppet. She was no puppet. I'm the puppet master, she thought. She stood, strong and proud and turned to Foxy. "Foxy," Tiger said. "Where're you going?"

"Far from here," replied Foxy.

"Thought you wanted to fight," she said looking at him smiling. Foxy looked back at Tiger and felt the strong Tiger who had saved his life was back.

"Yeah, and?" Foxy said.

"Well, I think your audience wants to know what we should do," Tiger said looking at Foxy then the crowd. Foxy smiled back at her and walked forward next to Tiger, looked out into the crowd and felt the fire in his belly. Tiger made sure the crowd was silenced by gazing at them, she need not have bothered you could hear a pin drop.

"Animals, I've had enough of these humans! Why do they drive us out of our homes?" Foxy cried. The animals looked at Foxy, he had their full attention. "Why do we run? I think they should be the ones to run don't you?" Foxy said as the crowd started to nod. "I'm tired of living my life in fear, they should fear us!" Foxy cried and the crowd became vocal in agreement with Foxy. "Who's tired of this way of life?" Foxy asked and was met with a unanimous roar from the crowd. "Foxy says, enough! I've had enough and you should too." The crowd shouted "enough" back at Foxy. "So are you with me?" The entire crowd replied, "yes". "Right then! Foxy says, let's take them out!" Foxy shouted. He had the crowd in his palm, whatever he said was a sure fire hit. Within seconds the whole of The Deep Jungle roared with cheers and the animals started chanting "FOXY, FOXY, FOXY, FOXY," it was a defining moment.

"Leopard!" Tiger shouted. "Assemble everyone. And I mean everyone. We take the fight to them tonight," Tiger said, not even considering her insubordination to The Elders with these actions. She felt proud and had got her fight back, her inner tiger.

"Yes my Queen," Leopard said with a nod, "But, what of The Elders?" Leopard asked.

"We say nothing. What are they going to do if all of us go? Nothing, that's what, I'm in charge," Tiger said confident that the 'government' would have no power if they decided to go it alone. "I'm sure you would agree with this course of action?" Tiger asked.

"Hot dang! Let's go!" Foxy interrupted and strolled off, oblivious to the pain that had only recently plagued his body.

12 – THE PREPARATION FOR BATTLE!

All the animals assembled. When Tiger gave the order to move out, she knew that the animals would need weapons. Whereas Tiger could use her canines, claws and general hunting skills to fight, an unarmed rabbit would not do very well when looking down the barrel of a hunter's shot gun, now would it?

In a clearing in The Jungle, a huge row of animals formed. Snakes, rabbits, monkeys, Dino, Donkey and Foxy were clutching long pieces of branch that they had obtained from the trees. Foxy was first to get a weapon of choice. The queue went back as far as the eye could see and at the front of the queue the warrior, or animal, was waiting for his or her stabbing weapon. Foxy handed in his implement of a two foot high stick and laid it on a high tree stump in front of him. Not too far above the tree stump was a hole in an adjacent tree. A woodpecker darted out and started pecking Foxy's stick as hard as it could. Foxy then rotated the stick, as the woodpecker hit it repeatedly, this formed a stabbing implement. Foxy could barely contain his excitement as his finished weapon was as sharp as a human's dagger.

"Awesome, Woodpecker. Just awesome!" Foxy commented and pulled out a piece of vine from his back that was burrowed in some fur. He tied one piece of the vine to one end of the stick and the other end to the sharper end. Foxy then placed it over his back and stood. Foxy kept his legs apart standing on his hind ones, and whipped his front legs over with his paws and lunged the stick in front of him.

"Foxy power," Foxy said and replaced it on his back. Foxy looked at the woodpecker and saw the other animals queuing up to get their stabbing implements too. Foxy turned and walked toward another clearing in The Deep Jungle when he heard a noise.

"You up there," the voice came from below Foxy. It was a very high pitched noise. Foxy looked around trying to see where the sound came from, "Ahoy down here," said the voice.

"What the?" Foxy said and looked down. A tortoise was there accompanied by a few other tortoises.

"I'm Tortoise," said the tortoise. "Me and my cousins have walked for a long, long time to help."

"Wow, I'm er grateful," Foxy said not really sure what they could do to help.

"Yes, pick me up will you?" Tortoise said. Foxy bent over and picked Tortoise up with his front paws.

"Okay, what now?" Foxy asked.

"Place me on your head," replied Tortoise. Foxy looked confused and moved the tortoise to his head. As Foxy did this, the head and legs of the tortoise shot in and revealed only a hard shiny shell. Foxy knew instantly how this would help.

"Tor-toise Power!" Foxy exclaimed. "Will this work?" Foxy asked.

"Course it will," came the reply as Tortoise's head sprang out for a second. "Head's up!" Tortoise cried and shot back in the shell. Foxy darted round and saw a pebble come flying at his head. Had Foxy not been wearing protection on his head he would've been knocked out, as it happened the pebble just bounced off the shell.

"Awesome!" Foxy shouted and looked over at who threw it. It was Dino who winked at Foxy. This is great! Foxy thought, believing even more that they had a chance.

"Me and my cousins will help you!" Tortoise said. The remaining tortoises formed a queue, as soon as the animals got their stabbing weapons, they could then come and get some armour in the form of a tortoise shell helmet. Foxy galloped off like a powerful stallion across the clearing and through some bramble where he saw some beavers working under the guidance of Leopard.

"What's going on here Leopard?" Foxy enquired.

"These workers are hollowing out some wood for us. Normally dam making is their game but look at this," said Leopard pointing with his nose to the Beaver's work.

"It looks like a giant spoon!" Foxy said.

"Exactly!" Leopard said. Foxy had no idea what this could possibly mean. He was right it did look like a spoon. It had a cylinder shaped not hollow handle and went to a hollowed out dip and certainly looked like a large wooden spoon. What an earth is that? Foxy thought.

"I'm sorry Leopard, I really cannot see it. What does it do?" Foxy asked.

"Hand me that coconut over there," Leopard said. Foxy trotted off a few yards and picked up a coconut and walked over to Leopard. "Now, put it on the spoon head as you call it." Foxy walked over and dropped it on the spoon head. "Stand back," Leopard ordered. With force Leopard jumped on the handle part of the spoon device and sent the coconut soaring high into the air.

"Hot dang!" Foxy shouted.

"Foxy, let me introduce to you the catapult!" Leopard replied.

"That's incredible, we can take out any henchmen who have height on us!"

"Preciscly!" Leopard exclaimed.

On the other side of The Deep Jungle, Tiger was with one of her tiger soldiers. She was sat overseeing the animals she had formed into an orderly line. There were monkeys, gorillas and boar in the queue but curiously they were carrying large leaves. The leaves were banana leaves and had a shape like a wide canoe and were a piercing emerald green in colour. A gorilla held one out in front of him like he was waiting for something to hit it. At the front of the queue was a large wild buffalo with its backside facing towards the gorilla. The gorilla walked close to the wild buffalo.

"Is this going to work?" Tiger's soldier asked.

"Wait and see," Tiger replied. The gorilla looked at Tiger and waited. Within seconds the wild buffalo let out an awesome 'Moo' noise like a cow and from its backside some wild buffalo dung came out steaming onto the rainforest leaf.

"That's grim!" Gorilla said.

"Indeed Gorilla," said Tiger. "But, with that level of methane gas in that poo, this'll be more powerful than any hunter's grenade!" Tiger proudly said.

"I'll take your word for it!" Gorilla replied and walked back, his arms still held out in front.

"Quickly Gorilla. Close the leaf to store as much gas as you can!" Tiger ordered. Gorilla closed the leaf with a noticeable grimace on his face. "Oh and one more thing Gorilla, get as many banana skins as you can. These will make excellent obstacles and traps for hunters to slip on," she said. Gorilla turned around and snapped at Tiger.

"Do I look like a chimp to you?" Gorilla snapped.

"You're a Gorilla," she replied.

"Yes a Gorilla, King Of The Gorillas, I'm not some chimp who chews on bananas all day." Gorilla replied angrily.

"Ok, then ask your chimp minions to bring them then, ok?" Tiger assertively said.

"Gruhhh," the gorilla said with obvious frustration and walked off with his front knuckles on his free arm pounding hard into the mud.

Tiger turned to the tiger that was with her. He was a Lieutenant grade of tiger.

"We'll need some stones to throw for the other animals, and more than that, some flint," Tiger said.

"Flint?" Lieutenant tiger asked.

"Yes, those dung leaves will not ignite themselves now, will they?" Tiger said.

"Indeed, my Queen. I'll see to it."

Foxy was running quickly and had a smile on his furry face. Not only was he content that everywhere he looked animals from all over, not just The Deep Jungle were preparing for battle, but he was kitted up to the max. He had his newfound friend on his head as a helmet for protection, his sharp stabbing stick tied onto his back, some dung bombs that he had also collected tied to a belt he had made from a stray vine around his waist, and what looked like a crossbow in his right hand. It was actually three pieces of stick. The first stick was just under a foot long that curved downward on one end that Foxy used as a handle. At the other end of the stick, Foxy had placed a curved stick on it, so it had an arc shape and secured it with some free vine. It looked like a crossbow except for the projection system which had an elastic band attached to it so in this respect it was more like a catapult. And with the crossbow what was Foxy's ammunition? Simple. Sharp hedgehog needles that he would pluck from a hedgehog that had also joined his cause and would sit in a pouch bag on Foxy's belt. Foxy would open the pouch and Hog would appear.

    "Reload Hog," said Foxy, as the hedgehog put his miniature paws over the bag and looked out with his tiny, beady eyes. Foxy would then pluck out some hairs, put them in the crossbow elastic, pull back and release!

    "There you go Foxy," Hog replied with a sweet friendly voice and then disappeared back into the pouch. Foxy ran to a large tree and saw his friends Dino and Donkey there. Dino was by a tree and up to something, mischief perhaps, while Donkey was at the foot of the tree looking up holding a bag in his teeth.

    "Yo, what're you two doing?" Foxy asked. Donkey turned around and looked at Foxy.

    "Jim! Dino hits tree hard Foxy," replied Donkey.

    "Why? What's up there?" Foxy asked. Foxy and Donkey looked up, it was a huge tree, thick and must have been over one hundred years old.

    "Almost got it!" Dino shouted at the foot of the tree and he repeatedly hit it with his head.

"Got what Dino? Anything good?" Foxy asked.

"I'd say Foxy!" Dino replied taking a long run up and ran at the tree.

"Jim!" Donkey cried.

"Almost, this will shift it, now yeah!" Dino crashed into the tree hard and fell on his bottom. The thud of force on the tree released a bee's nest that was up in the tree and the bees emerged from the nest and chased Foxy and Donkey.

"Move Donkey!" Foxy shouted.

"Jim!" Donkey replied as the two of them darted away in opposite directions. The bees started to attack Dino stinging him in delicate places. Dino ran in circles all around the tree. It was some time before the bees dispersed and Dino walked back to the tree and leant up against it. Foxy and Donkey walked up to Dino.

"You ok?" Foxy asked.

"Yeah, sore but look at this!" Dino said and scooped up the remaining bee nest. It was a large hive and honeycomb full of bees.

"Honey? Dino, now's not the time for food is it?" Foxy said.

"No, Foxy, the bees, this will drive those hunters mad, the stings, the buzz! Yeah? Yeah?" Dino said.

"Okay, that's cool! Let's group up with the others it must be time!" Dino took the hive bomb and placed it in Donkey's bag that was in Donkey's mouth, he then tied it and gave it back to Donkey to carry.

Moments later, Foxy, Dino, Donkey regrouped with Tiger and Crow, on her shoulder, who had assembled everyone outside her cave. Foxy walked up and stood proudly next to her and faced all the animals. Foxy looked at the proud strong Tiger and particularly liked her tiger stripes as they made her look powerful and would act as a good camouflage. What could I use? Foxy thought, he reached down and pawed at some mud and applied it to his face and body in striped motions to create war paint. Tiger looked at him.

"Hmm, I don't know if I should be offended or flattered Foxy," she said.

"Flattered, I'd say," Foxy replied.

"Offended actually," she replied. Foxy looked at her for a hint of a smile on her face. There was none but he decided to take a shot at a joke anyway. "Oh well, you can't make an omelette without breaking a few eggs!" Foxy said.

"Foxy," Tiger said with a slight grin on her face. The two of them looked out at the crowd. They were ready and Foxy could no longer contain his excitement.

"Look at me! Look at us! We're bad asses!" Foxy cried and then looked at Donkey realising he had insulted him with the 'ass' comment. He needn't have bothered. "Sorry Donkey. No offense." Foxy said.

"Jim?" Donkey asked in a confused manner. Foxy rolled his eyes and looked out at the army with Tiger.

"It's time," said Tiger, "let's finish it."

13 – THE PERIMETER OF THE CONGLOMERATE

The animals had walked for most of the night taking the path that Foxy, Tiger and Crow had taken earlier on their surveillance mission. It was still nightfall but within a few hours the dark night would lighten to reveal daylight. The big question was what daylight would it be? Would it a new dawn for the animals of The Deep Jungle and beyond? Or would it be the day The Conglomerate would spread itself deeper into The Jungle and get one step closer to total domination?

The perimeter of The Conglomerate was all too familiar to Foxy and seeing it for a second time brought a shiver up through his bony tail and to his spine. Foxy remembered the large industrial building as being cold, intimidating and made of steel. From the perimeter of The Conglomerate, you were not necessarily safe. Foxy took a look to his left and saw the remains of the tunnel he had dug only hours earlier with Tiger and Crow. This time they needed a plan of attack without being seen.

Tiger signalled to the animals to fall in, there must have been well over one hundred animals there and all armed to the teeth. Once all the animals were in front of Tiger, she revealed the plan.

"Okay… Crow is up there," she said and pointed with her paw to the sky. Crow was circling in the air and taking a mental note of all hunters and henchman patrolling The Conglomerate. "Crow will alert us the minute something is wrong," she said.

"Look…" Dino said, "at… the… way… he… flies… it's… so… mesmer…" Dino was not able to finish his sentence as he fell asleep mesmerised. Foxy stepped in and lightly slapped him around the face. "What? Who?" Dino said. Tiger gave Dino a look that could pierce metal. Dino shrugged his shoulders apologetically, "Sorry, Tiger."

"First things first. Lieutenant!" Tiger called to her most capable tiger. The Lieutenant ran forward. "I've a special job for you."

"What is thy bidding my Queen?" asked the Lieutenant with a slightly bowed head.

"In case we get seen ahead, or if any of us get pinned down on the way to the entrance, we're going to need some cover," Tiger said. "I want you and some animals of your choosing to hold here and use the catapult to attack any hunters that are attacking us from high up as we run on the ground."

"It will be done my Queen," the Lieutenant replied and took a step back. He then ran backwards through the crowd to assemble a team.

"Ok, Foxy and I will go the farthest oil drum and then make our way inside after igniting it. Dino and Donkey, you get to the nearest one," Tiger said.

"Remember animals, once they are ignited, make your way into the heart of The Conglomerate and take down any humans that stand in your way," Foxy said.

"Yes," Tiger added. "And remember, take no prisoners! It is them or us. What's it going to be?" Tiger asked rhetorically. Tiger looked at all the animals and made a judgement call. "Split yourselves in half. Half with Team A that is Foxy and I, the rest of you with Team B, Dino and Donkey."

"Why is Dino part of Team B? Surely any team Dino is in will be the A Team, Team A right?" Dino asked.

"Does it really matter?" Foxy butted in.

"Easy for you to say Foxy, you're in Team A," Dino replied.

"Who gives a bin what team you're in?" Foxy replied frustrated.

"Well, okay Foxy you are now Team B and Donkey and I are Team A okay? Dino suggested.

"What?" Foxy asked. "Give me strength."

"There is no trade, what do you think this is? A food exchange?" Tiger said angrily.

"I just thought," said Dino.

"Well don't. You're Team B and we're Team A, is that understood? Tiger asked with a hint of venom.

"Sure, okay sorry Tiger, let's continue," Dino said

"Never mind telling me to get on with it. Tiger will get on with it when she's good and ready," Tiger cried.

"Sure, Okay. I'm wrong, let's forget it."

"Grrrr," she replied. Dino took a step back and then whispered into Donkey's ear.

"But we are Team A, right Donkey," Dino said whilst lightly elbowing Donkey in the ribs.

"Jim?" Donkey replied. Foxy had heard Dino's whisper with his heightened hearing, as did Tiger. Foxy shook his head and rolled his eyes as Tiger sighed.

"Give me strength indeed," Tiger said to Foxy.

"I know," Foxy replied.

"Right, as I was saying Crow will signal when it's time to move in," Tiger said looking up. Dino also looked up at Crow.

"What's the signal Tiger?" Dino asked. Tiger said nothing and smiled, Foxy stepped back. Dino carried on staring into the night air mesmerised by Crow's elegant flying. Dino opened his mouth, almost in a trance and his head circled round mimicking the pattern that Crow was making. "Okay... Tiger... Dino... waiting..."

Suddenly, Dino's face got covered in bird's droppings from Crow.

"Jim!" Donkey cried in confusion. Foxy jumped up and drew his sharpened stick stabbing implement.

"That's the signal! Let's go!" Foxy cried.

The animals ran down a hill that levelled out and then went on a gradual incline. Foxy and Tiger veered to the left with many animals, while Donkey and Dino veered even farther to the left and the remaining animals went with them.

The perimeter edge was now in Foxy and Tiger's grasp as they approached the high steel fence that had barbed wire at the top of it. Tiger ran straight into the fence and the sheer power of her run made her go straight through it. Foxy on the other hand, could not rely on such brute force due to his lack of size. Foxy took his stabbing weapon and lowered it into the floor whilst running, and like a pole vaulter, used it to hoist himself high into the air whilst expertly grabbing a hold of the pole. The laws of physics did not come into play here, how Foxy managed to clear the fifteen foot plus high fence using only two feet and a bit pole is not explainable, but he did clear the fence easily.

"My way was better," said Tiger as she came to a stop on the other side of the fence.

"Yeah yeah," replied Foxy.

"Why didn't you just go under it whilst digging Foxy? Did you want to impress me or something?" Tiger said with a hint of jest.

"No, no, no Foxy just wanted to try something new, broaden his skills," Foxy replied.

"Right," Tiger said. Crow had done a great job with the signal, his timing was impeccable. How he managed to get the animals to run in the blind spots of the hunters and video surveillance equipment at the right moment was something to be in awe of. Foxy and Tiger ran to the outer wall of The Conglomerate and stood on their hind legs with their backs pressed against the cold steel and slid along it. When they reached one end of the wall, they went around and saw what they came for, two large oil drums.

"Here they are, Foxy," Tiger said.

"Alright. Hang on a second," he replied and put his paw down to his belt, his foxy utility belt with all his newly made gadgets and grabbed one of the banana leaves with fresh wild buffalo dung and unclipped it off of his belt. He let the leaf rest on one paw as he pulled out two pieces of flint stone from another pouch bag compartment on his belt. Foxy needed another paw as he had to ignite the leaf dung bomb.

"Here hold this," Foxy said handing the dung bomb to Tiger.

"I beg your pardon?" Tiger replied, insulted that Foxy had asked her to hold something that had come out of an animal's bottom.

"What?" Foxy replied.

"That Foxy. You really expect me, Queen Of The Jungle to hold that?"

"Yesh."

"No chance, fox!"

"Tiger, just for a minute. This was your idea the leaf dung bombs!"

"Yes only for animals like yourselves that require weapons. Tiger needs not weapons," she said and then showed her canine teeth and claws, "Tiger only needs these and these as weapons."

"Give me strength."

"You're on your own Foxy."

"Fine. Jeesh, I will figure it out." He took the dung bomb in his right paw, walked up to one of the oil barrels and threw his paw hard into the oil drum so the bomb would stick to it. Sure enough it did, although an excess amount of dung came spewing out of the sides and went in Tiger's direction and almost hit her.

"Lucky for you that didn't hit me Foxy," she roared. Foxy planted another dung bomb on the remaining drum. Foxy took his paws and stroked them together to clean his paws from the filth. He picked up two pieces of flint and prepared to bash them together. Foxy paused and realised that this moment, or the few after it could be his last and wanted to thank Tiger for believing in him and risking her life to help him.

"You know... Tiger I..." Foxy said unable to convey exactly what he was feeling at that moment. He need not have bothered. Tiger knew exactly what was happening and also felt proud of not only Foxy but herself.

"I know," replied Tiger.

"Let's finish it," Foxy responded and took a deep breath and looked into the early morning, still dark sky that was greying. After a short while Foxy hit the two pieces of flint together but nothing happened. It took a few more attempts before a spark went flying off of one of the pieces of flint and straight onto the banana leaf.

"Wow, they go up quickly," Foxy remarked.

"No time to admire it Foxy, let's go now these drums will go up sooner than you can say…" Tiger's sentence was cut off by a large noise of a siren. The alarm had been set off by The Conglomerate.

"Darn, I'd thought we'd have longer," Tiger said. "If a hunter gets here in time they could remove the dung bombs." Tiger noted.

"You said they would explode sooner than…" Foxy asked.

"That's before the alarm went off. We don't have time to wait now," she replied.

"Okay, give me that paper on the floor quickly," Foxy ordered. Tiger picked it up in her jaws and gave it to Foxy who took it in his paw and put it on the slow flame that was forming on the oil drum. Foxy then scrambled up the oil drum to the top of it and stood next to an exhaust pipe that was leading into the drum.

"Strange," Tiger said, "I didn't know foxes can climb things?"

"This fox is quarter grey and three thirds red fox, Tiger. Greys can climb trees," Foxy said proudly.

"But oil drums? Okay, but can one third grey and the rest red foxes hurry up and climb down as quickly as they climbed up?"

"Yesh," he replied and turned and threw the ignited paper into the exhaust pipe and jumped down. Foxy and Tiger ran away from the oil drums towards the entrance of The Conglomerate, Foxy spotted some hunters on the levels above them in The Conglomerate ready to fire at them. Foxy pulled out his crossbow and prepared to aim. Foxy was beaten by the hunter as the hunter got a shot off that ricocheted off of Foxy's tortoise helmet.

"That was lucky," Foxy said as Tortoise, popped his head and arm out momentarily to give a smile and a 'paws up'.

"Reload!" Foxy shouted and from his belt appeared the hedgehog with the beady eyes and smile, curled into a ball. Foxy plucked out some sharp needles from the hog and put them in his crossbow elastic launching mechanism, pointed at the hunters and pulled back the elastic and released it. As the needles went into the air they caught two of the hunters in their backsides causing them to drop their rifles and hold onto their bottoms, crying with agony.

"Bulls eye!" Tiger said. "Nice shot, Foxy!"

"Foxy power," he cockily replied. Within seconds the oil drums they had just left ignited, creating a huge explosion that left a mushroom cloud as if there was nuclear explosion in the distance. The explosion would start a chain reaction of explosions into The Conglomerate structure. Foxy and Tiger ran into The Conglomerate, right through the front door and were joined by Crow who took his place on Tiger's right shoulder.

Meanwhile, on the other side of the perimeter, Donkey and Dino were struggling to ignite the oil drums. The Conglomerate structure was powered by four oil drums and Foxy and Tiger had taken out two on one side. If these were taken out, that would cripple The Conglomerate of any power as well as security they had inside the structure.

"Darn it!" Dino cursed, as he was furiously rubbing two sticks together trying to ignite a spark onto the dung grenades they had managed to attach to the drums. "I knew we should've used stone and not wood, Donkey!"

"Jim!" Donkey unhelpfully replied. Dino continued at a ferocious pace to create a spark. His hoofs were gripping the sticks very tightly and eventually one of the sticks snapped, making Dino very frustrated.

"Oh darn it!" Dino shouted and threw the sticks away angrily. Dino huffed and puffed a few times, then his eyes lit up. "Stand back all! I will create fire from my Dino lungs!" The animals looked at each other in a state of shock. Did this hippo truly believe he could spew flames from his mouth? Dino inhaled deeply, his body grew in size and his lungs filled with air. "AROOOOOOOAAAAAAAAHHH!" Dino shouted and breathed out with nothing more than warm breath and no fire.

The rest of Team B looked on in astonishment and some scratched their heads. Dino paused and lowered his head not sure what had happened.

"What? I don't understand," Dino said.

"What's there to not understand? You can't breathe fire!" Leopard cried.

"Yes I can, I am Dino, Lord Dino!" Dino roared convincing no one. The animals looked at each other somewhat embarrassed.

"Unbelievable, move aside you two morons," said Leopard as he strolled past Dino and Donkey to a rabbit who was carrying a pouch in his mouth. "Give me some flint will you?" Leopard asked.

"Jim! Dino, tries again, Dino can do it," Donkey said encouraging Dino to not give up. Dino turned and faced the drum and looked at it.

"You know you're right Donkey, I am Dino, hear me roar!" Dino shouted. Leopard meanwhile placed some flint between his front paws and looked at the rabbit. Leopard nodded to the rabbit, and then the rabbit kicked a piece of flint towards the flint that Leopard was holding. A perfect spark formed and flew just over Dino's head towards the dung bombs on the drums.

"ARRRRRRROOOOOOOOOOOOOOOOOOOOOOOOOOOOOOOOOOAAAAAAAAAAAAAAAAAAAHHHHHHHHHHHH!" Dino screamed and breathed out. The spark was still flying in the air and hit the dung bomb head on and ignited it. The flame formed, the bomb was ignited.

"Jim! Dino did it!" Donkey cried.

"Grraarrr, Lord Dino, does it again," roared Dino very proud of himself. Leopard shook his head and walked in front of Dino.

"Alright, animals move out!" Leopard ordered with authority. Dino, not too impressed by being usurped as leader repeated the order to get some authority back.

"Yes animals, you heard the Leopard, let's go!" Dino called.

As Dino, Donkey and Leopard ran forward with their entourage of animals behind them, they noticed the mud in the ground start flying up. There were hunters on the roof of The Conglomerate firing down on them with rifles.

"Darn, how many up there?" Dino asked.

"Hard to tell, take cover!" Leopard shouted as they all ran and jumped over a mud mound on the way to the entrance of The Conglomerate.

"This is no good, we're sitting ducks here!" Dino cried. As he said this a duck, who was part of the group took insult at the comment.

"Quack, Quack!" Duck said.

"Sorry," replied Dino. Leopard peered over the mound to have a look.

"There's three hunters up there, they're firing in panic. The explosion from Team A must've scared them a bit," Leopard said.

"You mean Team B," replied Dino.

"Whatever Dino," Leopard said rolling his eyes. "Still, we can't stay here too long or we will be duck pate."

"QUACK!" Duck protested.

"Where did this duck come from?" Dino asked.

"It doesn't matter. Come on Lieutenant, don't you let me down now," said Leopard lying flat behind the mound clutching his head with his paws.

Back at the perimeter the tiger Lieutenant held ground. He was with a team of animals, a rabbit, the Gorilla and a monkey.

"Load 'em up!" the Lieutenant shouted. The animals had quite a nifty system to do this. It consisted of the monkey hurling a coconut from a pile he was standing on to the feet of the rabbit. Once the rabbit received them, he would kick them with his large feet with a 'thump' on the floor, and the coconut would land on the spoon shaped dip of the catapult. This was repeated a few times until the Lieutenant was satisfied and then he would give the order to fire.

"Fire!" The Lieutenant shouted.

"Aye," Gorilla replied and jumped high into the air and his three hundred plus pounds of muscular weight came crashing down on the launch handle end to propel the coconuts high into the air towards the hunters. Three coconuts went flying into the air; two of them narrowly missed one of the hunters who resorted to lying prone on the floor.

"That hunter's lying down!" Lieutenant cried. "Load me up another five coconuts this time."

Monkey threw a coconut to rabbit, rabbit kicked it on the platform and this was repeated a further four times, they now had five on the spoon dip of the catapult.

"Lock and load!" Gorilla shouted. Lieutenant looked with narrow eyes at the hunter and waited a bit. He could see the hunter, who was not firing, get up and start to take aim on Team B.

"Fire," the Lieutenant calmly said. As Gorilla jumped on the platform with the same amount of force as before, five coconuts went flying high in the air. This time, two did not miss, three did not miss, not even four. Five coconuts landed squarely on the hunter, two in his face, one in his stomach knocking all the wind out of him and two by his shins.

"ARRGGGHGH!" The hunter screamed, dropping his rifle and falling from the roof of The Conglomerate down to the floor to a certain death.

Behind the mound, Leopard smiled and realised that with one hunter not firing and more coconuts on their way, Team B could move forward to the entrance of The Conglomerate.

"Lieutenant, my old buddy, I knew you'd not let me down," Leopard smiled. "Team, roll out run to the entrance of The Conglomerate! Go, go, go, and go!"

Team B emerged from behind the mound and ran towards the entrance, but as they were running the shooting started from two other hunters. Leopard was not worried, he knew his 'back' was covered and the firing from the hunters stopped as the hunters had to take cover from the onslaught of coconuts coming their way.

As Team B entered the building, quite a way behind Foxy and Tiger, they heard another explosion from the outside. The oil drums had exploded and had sent a chain reaction of fire into The Conglomerate. The Conglomerate was now crippled of any power and security; this was a major blow for The Conglomerate. However, each animal knew this meant little if they did not put an end to the people behind this corporate nightmare. The Conglomerate could always rebuild.

The final battle would be fought right here right now.

14 – THE BOSS BATTLES IN THE CONGLOMERATE!

"What on earth was that?" Gore shouted in his office in the middle of the night. He stood in front of his desk with the two doorways to either side, alarmed by the explosions and The Conglomerate's loss of power, evident from the darkness in the office and the secure door locks now broken. The explosion had created many fires from within, and Gore's office, while safe for the moment being on the top floor, would certainly burn and perish if he could not do something quickly.

"The whole place is going up," said Toad as he spat on the floor. Rat came in from one of the doorways in a very camp way and caught Gore's gaze and frustration.

"Rat, stop mincing about and do something! Go to auxiliary power!" Gore ordered.

"Auxiliary circuit's destroyed Master," said Rat waving his arms around.

"GRRRR," screamed Gore, "Then do something else. We should've attacked them first! Rat, do something quickly or face redundancy from The Conglomerate!" Gore walked behind his desk leaving the usual trail of goo under his robe as he walked. Rat ran to the doorway from where he had entered.

What on earth is happening? Gore thought to himself, confused and in a state of bewilderment. He went to sit down to collect his thoughts and looked over at Toad. The look on Toad's face said it all, neither of them had a plan.

There was a noise by the large double door to Gore's office. The noise vanished, then reappeared again. The noise was accompanied by the double doors effortlessly flapping open like saloon doors in an American Western movie. Something came through the doors, something grotesque, smelly and bloody. It was a human, half bitten to death and the pieces slid along the floor easily, aided by Gore's gooey residue. It landed at the foot of the desk. Gore walked round from behind his desk to look at the human remains. It was a hunter, one of his loyal protectors, one of his guards.

"What…" Gore said unable to finish his sentence as Tiger and Foxy ran in. Tiger looked serious on all fours while Foxy stood upright on his hind legs. He still had his helmet and war attire on and pointed his sharpened stick ready for battle. The sharpened stick had red on the tip, it was clear that Foxy had been putting the stick to good use.

"There's a lot more of this going on outside this office and throughout The Conglomerate and even the perimeter! We're here to finish this now and put an end to your tyranny and evil ways," said Tiger.

"A frog! You mean to tell me a frog is in charge? A human does not run the show?" Foxy asked a bit shocked. Gore was not in a good mood and slowly raised his arms and pulled back his long sleeves that would not look out of place on a wizard's arm. Toad took a step to his right to give Gore some breathing space and waited.

"Ah, the famous fox. And what have we here? A Tiger?" Gore said. "Look at my hands, I am not an animal I am a human being," screamed Gore showing his webbed hands.

"Yesh, Yesh, whatever fatty," replied Foxy.

"Indeed," Tiger replied.

"What say you Toad? It's been a while since we skinned a Tiger? Would be a good investment in the marketplace some Tiger skin," said Gore looking to Toad who nodded in approval with a bowed head. "And, as for the fox, well that will be nothing really, that will be… how do you say… fun."

"Talk all you want frog. It's over, you're finished." Tiger said.

"HAHAHAH!" Toad began to laugh uncontrollably and Gore looked at him with a wry smile.

"You must excuse Toad but something appears to have tickled his sense of humour," Gore cried as Crow flew in and found his position on Tiger's right shoulder. He had a status update of the mission and was ready to feed back to Tiger.

"Squark. Squuuuuuuarrrrrrrk. Squarrrrk. Sqwarrrrrrkkkkkkk. Squark. Squark! Squaarrrrrrrrrrrrkkk! SQUARRRRRRK," said Crow reporting to Tiger effectively on the mission's status. Tiger nodded in agreement, Foxy narrowed his eyes and also nodded.

"I couldn't agree more with you Crow and this is good news indeed," said Tiger.

"Well," Gore said, "Well Tigress, what did he say?" Foxy slapped his forehead with his paw at Gore's question. Foxy had made a similar mistake when he first met Tiger to call her Tigress. She did not like that name before and she certainly did not like it now, it did nothing to further female tiger kind.

"Now you've gone and done it, frog," said Foxy, "Tigress? She's a tiger!"

"Oh, a tiger, Well excuse me. TIGER what did he say?" Gore asked sarcastically.

"Well, it kinda gets lost in translation, but apart from the fact that all our animals are tearing up all humans in The Conglomerate, if I was to translate the rest into a language you would understand then Crow said that humans, in particular the fat Toad over there, have a saying. A word of four letters, and you are full of it!" Tiger roared.

"SQUARK SQUARK!" Crow laughed, spread his wings wide and brought them back together again mimicking clapping.

"Enough!" Gore shouted. "This ends now," he said raising his arm.

"I want the frog," Foxy said raising his stick ready for action.

"Suits me fine. Have you ever had a frog in your throat? It's not nice I can assure you," Tiger replied. The constant frog jibes were getting to Gore, with each new insult his brow creased from the stress.

"Yep, many times Tiger, I've had a frog in my throat, but not one as fat as this. This frog's for the taking and Foxy's the taker," replied Foxy.

"Toad and frog… How confusing. Fine, I'll take the fat Toad," she said.

"HAHAH! Toad, let's take them out!" Gore ordered as a Mexican standoff ensued. Foxy and Tiger stood side by side together as Gore and Toad mirrored them.

Tiger roared into action prematurely leaping onto Toad. As she was about to land, Toad pulled out a sword concealed in a slit down the side of his left trouser leg and took a wild swing. The swing was right on target, the tip of the blade caught Tiger across her chest leaving a dark red blood stripe that would certainly scar.

"Ouch. Now Toad, why'd you have to go and do that? I've got enough stripes on my body," Tiger said with fire in her eyes. The pain was nothing to Tiger. If the wound would indeed scar I will have another story to tell, thought Tiger.

"Come on Tiger!" Toad cried and held his left arm out long with the right arm held back, bent at the elbow. He lowered his body so his legs were in a squat.

Foxy stared at Gore and wondered how he would attack this man who was more than five feet taller than his two foot something. Foxy dug his left paw forward into the ground and shifted the weight on his right hind paw. Foxy's front paws were holding the stabbing implement, he was ready to strike but not before checking on Tiger. Stupid fox, she can take care of herself, Foxy mentally cursed to himself. But he was right to check. Tiger was being led backwards, Toad was swinging his sword like a wild man. There was zero precision in his wild swings; all he was achieving was getting Tiger to fall back across the other side of the room away from Foxy. Sooner or later Toad would run out of energy and Tiger would strike her pray, Foxy thought.

Foxy lunged at Gore with his stabbing stick.

"Hairless tailed fox! You are no match for me!" Gore screamed. Gore to Foxy's surprise, was very athletic for someone so large. As Foxy stabbed, Gore masterfully sidestepped and grabbed Foxy's arm with his left arm straight, picked him up and threw him using his right arm with more force in the centre of the room.

"Hahah!" Gore laughed as he walked calmly behind his desk. He bent over and started rotating a lever clockwise. The area Foxy was on elevated about thirty feet in the air creating a raised circled platform with a large fall. Gore came out from behind the desk and bent his knees down and lunged high into the air, jumping a staggering thirty feet onto the platform. Foxy was impressed.

"As you so noted fox, I do look like a frog. This is a result of a genetic mutation. There are some positive side effects, such as the ability to jump high." Gore walked toward Foxy on the far end of the elevated platform. The elevated platform was about twenty feet by twenty feet.

Meanwhile, Tiger was still biding her time. Toad would swipe towards her paws but Tiger would leap over the swipes. If Toad swiped at her head she would lie on all fours and avoid the blow. Toad was becoming very predictable while Tiger was serious and calm.

"Annoying tiger," said Toad, "stand still." Tiger stood prone. Toad puffed and wheezed, clearly tired from all the exercise and spat on the floor. "Good," he said as Tiger sat as if she was a stone statue. Toad took a mighty swing with all his might. Tiger yawned, took a side step and lifted her right paw and scraped all down Toad's face from top to bottom. Toad, dropped his sword and brought his hands to his face, wiped and then looked at his blood soaked hands.

"My face!" You pesky cat, I'll make you suffer!" Toad screamed and charged towards Tiger with the same erratic behaviour that had got his face scratched. Tiger smiled revealing her canines, her tactics were working. Toad was exhausted, running on empty.

"Stay still," panted Toad.

If Foxy and Tiger had a plan of ordering the remaining members of Team A to take down any humans they came across while Foxy and Tiger took down the two head leads, then one would be forgiven for thinking that Team B had a similar plan seeing as Dino and Donkey themselves were on their own. The truth of the matter was that Leopard had taken the rest of Team B to secure the area.

"Donkey scared," said Donkey as he and Dino walked along a corridor tunnel that was dark. The two of them had no idea where in The Conglomerate they were, they only knew they were somewhere in the basement.

"It's okay Donkey. There's no one here," replied Dino as they walked further along the dark corridor that widened out. At the end of the corridor of stone and brickwork, there was a more spacious area, still of brick but in the shape of a cylinder very much like a castle turret. There appeared to be light at the end of the tunnel, not from electricity but from candles. There was a dripping noise of water that was hitting a puddle in the open area and behind the puddle was a wooden cage.

"What's that?" Donkey asked.

"A cage," replied Dino, "Looks like a cage and it's not empty. This is a dungeon. Gosh, I hope they didn't get Foxy or Tiger."

"Jim!" Donkey screamed, but this was no nervous tick of his condition and Dino knew immediately that Donkey was making a statement with full control over his verbal patterns, it really was Jim and Jim wasn't alone. Donkey leapt on his hind legs and stood upright, something he rarely does.

"It *is* Jim!" Dino shouted, surprised and quite impressed that he recognised someone he had never met but had heard so much about, albeit indirectly. Jim was an infant donkey, very small and starved looking. Like his father, he had a bluish, brown coat with large ears, and was resting in the wooden cage, shivering from the cold of this basement dungeon. Jim was desperately trying to get warm by lying under his mother's legs. Jill, Donkeys wife and Jim's mother looked gaunt and undernourished. Her blue coat had become thin from the trauma of being a prisoner. Donkey wondered why on earth they were here. Donkey knew what the community was saying in his part of The Jungle, that his wife and child had run away due to his boring nature and dim-wittedness. The Tourette's that Donkey had was a result of them leaving and he always knew that if he saw them again his condition would improve. However, his intelligence would not improve until he got himself some common sense. Donkey's mind was going a million miles an hour, they were captured but why?

"Donkey, don't come here it's a trap!" Jill shouted to Donkey.

"Jim! Jill!" Donkey shouted, unable to control himself as he galloped forward towards them.

"Donkey no!" Dino screamed, but it was too late. Rat emerged from the shadows of the dull, dark and damp dungeon and jumped on a switch in the stone floor and pulled a lever. Donkey found himself entrapped in another cage that came crashing down from the ceiling high up in the dungeon turret.

"HAHAH. Stupid Donkey! Fell right into my rat trap. Oh the irony," said the camp Rat, rather proud as he danced to himself, walking backwards sliding his feet on the floor.

"Stupid Rat!" Dino shouted with venom, his spit coming out of his baggy jowls.

"Watch your step hippo," said Rat and clung onto the lever ready to pull again.

"How much are they paying you? Huh Rat?" Dino asked with disgust.

"Not much, but this will get me a promotion," said Rat, "I work for The Conglomerate until I die."

"That day may be closer than you think. I hope it was worth it, to turn your back on your own people," Dino commented.

"You have no idea," said Rat smiling. "The perks of working for The Conglomerate are beyond your wildest dreams. In exchange for zero free time, I get full private healthcare! I get two annual bonuses, I get a car allowance and I can't even drive. All of my food is paid as I charge it to expenses for make believe business dinners. I get free drinks, business trips. I stay late to make it appear I'm doing work so my manager rewards me! I come up with marketing terms that mean nothing to anyone yet they still nod as if they understand! I give work to others to complete and pass it off as my own! Sure, I'll get stress and grow old before my time but I get respect. My own people! You must be joking, none of you ever treated me with any respect!" The rat spat on the floor, "you're all blinkered idiots. The Conglomerate is taking over, and I was offered a chance of greatness and I seized it."

"Why keep prisoners?" Dino asked.

"These are part of an experiment. Lord Gore is obsessed with experiments. He wants to eradicate all animal kind but first wants to try a bit of genetic experimentation."

"Today is the day you die rat," said Dino.

"Stupid hippo. Do you really think The Conglomerate left me alone to set this trap with no weapons?" Rat looked around him and realised that actually, yes, The Conglomerate had done just that. The rat was alone with just this trap and no weapons. As Rat looked back at Dino, Dino could not contain himself anymore and started laughing loud as his belly fat moved up and down like waves in The Red Sea.

"Well," laughed Dino, "it really seems that when it comes down to it, The Conglomerate cares little for its employees' well-being and more for its profits, wouldn't you say so Rat?" Dino joked.

"I... erm... stand over there will you hippo?" Rat said in an act of desperation to get Dino in a sweet spot on the floor so he could activate his rat trap.

"No," laughed Dino.

"Erm... right... yes, that's it. Move one step and you will forever be frozen..." Dino raised his hoof to Rat and stood on his hind legs, the sheer height of Dino brought a newfound terror to Rat. Rat started to tremble with fear.

"Rat," said Dino, "I hate to interrupt you but, there are more pressing engagements at hand."

"Yeah?" Rat asked, "like what you fat hippo?"

"It's dinner time, can you not hear the chimes of dinner?" Dino said, the chimes he spoke of being his internal body clock. "My stomach is growling."

"Huh?" Rat asked.

"GET IN MY BELLY!" Dino shouted and charged at Rat. Rat screamed uncontrollably and shivered as his jaw got lower and lower and almost hit the floor with fear. As Dino ran over on his hind legs, the thump of weight in the floor made Rat bounce up and down and Dino caught Rat on one of the bounces and picked him up and instantly swallowed him whole, no chewing or anything.

"YUCK!" Dino proclaimed, "how does Foxy eat such things! Tastes like a rat!"

"Dino! Help Jim!" Donkey cried. Dino felt nauseous having eaten such a horrible snack.

"Deary me, what have I done? All my hard work dieting and being an herbivore to get my slim frame back. And now, now I'm fat again due to this carnivorous weakness that has injected itself back in me. Curse this protein addiction that never left me!" Dino cried.

"Dino! Please help Jim and Jill?" Donkey asked his friend.

"What? Oh yes of course Donkey, forgive me," said Dino and ran over to the wall and pushed the lever upwards to raise the cage that Jill and Jim were in.

"Jim!" Donkey shouted as the cage lifted free from Jim and Jill. Shortly after, the cage that had trapped Donkey also raised.

"There you go," smiled Dino, and Donkey ran on all fours and hugged Jim and embraced Jill with a hug.

"Jim! Jim!" Donkey cried.

"Oh Donkey, it's so good to see you!" Jill said with tears in her eyes.

"Jim!" Donkey shouted, the Tourette's not quite having left him yet.

"Aw shucks," said Dino overcome with emotion. He wiped his chunky hoof to his face to swipe away a rogue tear falling down his cheek.

Meanwhile, all was not going well for Foxy. Every lunge, every swipe and every stab with his stick was being parried masterfully by Gore's bare hands. Foxy calmed himself, caught his breath while Gore laughed. Foxy reached into a pouch on his combat belt and pulled out some stones and threw them with little precision.

"Let's see you dodge this frog," said the cocky fox. Gore blocked two of the stones with each of his hands, two more stones missed him completely but one caught him square on the head. It momentarily stunned Gore and Foxy seized the opportunity by running forward, spinning his stabbing implement three hundred and sixty degrees and stabbed Gore right in his fat belly.

"Urgh," said Gore, as Foxy smiled. Foxy's celebration was short lived as the wound produced nothing but green slime out of the puncture. Gore shoved Foxy backwards with one hand, pulled the stick free with his other hand and threw it thirty metres down off of the platform. "Now you've done it fox," cried Gore, and lunged at Foxy with his right arm. He caught Foxy around the neck and squeezed hard before adding his left hand for more pressure, lifting Foxy clean off of the floor. Foxy struggled for breath and looked over off of the side to see how Tiger was getting on. Foxy was relieved to see Tiger was ok, but knew for him, this breath could be his last.

Toad was still swinging like a madman, dripping with sweat and out of breath.

"Pesky Tiger," Toad said gasping for air, "I got... I got... I've nothing left," he cried.

"Good!" Tiger replied, smiled and leapt at him with all her force to floor him. She did not even let Toad scream and proceeded to feast on his stomach and ripped his intestines out. Toad died instantly. "Insolent Toad," said Tiger as she crawled off him, her only wound being the swipe across her chest at the beginning of the brawl. "I hate a human or so called Toad in the throat more than a frog," she said and stopped in her tracks. A frog, she thought, how is Foxy doing? Tiger looked up and saw Foxy being strangled to death and proceeded to run towards the platform, thirty metres up, but not even she, with her strength could scale that height in a short space of time. "Foxy!" Tiger shouted at the top of her voice with great concern.

Foxy's face turned redder than children's tomato ketchup sauce.

"Grarrrrr!" Foxy cried.

"You are dead fox! You'll never finish The Conglomerate!" Gore said.

"You... we... destroyed... you... today," said Foxy with some triumph.

"Ha, we will rebuild, we are like software you fool we just reload," Gore replied, giving Foxy an idea. Moments ago, Foxy was contemplating death and how actually this would be a good death, but now his ears had pricked up more than they ever had. What Gore said about software and reloading made Foxy think of something. Sure, Foxy had no idea what software was but he could read between what was said. If he could pull this off he might just live through this.

"You'll... never... reload," Foxy said, his last word muffled.

"Come again?" Gore asked unable to hear what Foxy had said.

"I said, RELOAD!" This time the words were not muffled, they were crystal clear and on Foxy's belt the small head of Hog appeared and looked up with his beady eyes. He quickly got into position and bent forward and squeezed to reload Foxy's crossbow catapult himself. As Hog squeezed, only one pine needle came out his skin. It would have to be enough and Foxy reached down with his paw and pulled back the catapult and released it. Talk about a shot in the dark, but it was all he had. The needle flew from the catapult and hit Gore right on his fat bulbous foot.

"GRRRARRRR my toe!" Gore screamed and dropped Foxy to hold his foot. Foxy caught his breath as Gore hopped around the platform clutching his foot in pain.

"We'll never finish The Conglomerate? That's what you think frog. FOXXXXYYYY POWWWWWWWWWEEEEERRRR!" Foxy shouted and leapt high in the air and twisted his body around and let his bony tail come arcing around to catch Gore from shoulder to hip in a diagonal motion. The force of the move created a blinding light that caused Tiger to stop in her tracks and cover her eyes on the ground with her paws. On the platform, Gore was also blinded by the light, unsure of what had happened. He settled himself for a few moments and then started to laugh,

"HAHAHA. Foxy Power? Foxy Power you say? Where's your bushy tail? You missed me fox! You missed me!" Gore screamed like a maniac.

"Did I?" Foxy replied, his cockiness and confidence back as he stood arms folded on his hind legs. Gore looked at Foxy and then opened his mouth to speak but nothing came out. There was a frothy liquid emerging from his body and this time it was bloody, very bloody. The bony tail of Foxy had cut Gore clean in half from shoulder to hip. The weight of Gore's upper body buckled the lower part and he slumped to a heap on the floor.

"Gulp," was the last word spoken by Gore as he lay motionless. His whole body melted instantly in front of Foxy. The residue of liquid poured over the sides of the platform and found its way deep into the grooves in the floor.

"Foxy Power," said Foxy and jumped down the platform some thirty feet below to where Tiger was, who came running up to him.

"Alright?" Tiger asked.

"I'll live. You?" Foxy replied.

"No sweat," she smiled and Crow flew back in on her shoulder.

"Squawk!" Crow said.

"Yes, Crow. Foxy?"

"Yesh?"

"Hop on Foxy," Tiger said showing her back.

"Foxy care not for ride," Foxy replied still acting proud as punch.

"Maybe, but it's for the best, this whole place is coming down. Let's go!" Tiger was right. The whole of The Conglomerate was falling apart, they would be quicker if Foxy rode on her back.

"Yes ma'am!" Foxy said and back flipped onto her back. Tiger proceeded to run on all fours with Crow on her shoulder and Foxy in the saddle, so to speak. The building was on fire and falling down around them. Tiger leapt over an obstacle in her path as she headed out of Gore's main room and down the spiral staircase. If at any time Tiger encountered an obstacle, she would just jump it. Occasionally Foxy would tug on her skin by her neck to tell her to jump like a jockey on a horse would.

By the time Tiger got Crow, Foxy and herself to the ground floor, the whole of The Conglomerate was up in smoke and Tiger ran towards the front doors and leapt at them. The doors were so weak that they crumbled under the force, and as she got outside she had to squint a bit as there was now sunlight in the pale blue morning sky.

Outside The Conglomerate were the animals that had joined our heroes on their quest and they all filed in behind Tiger who kept running as she cleared the perimeter of The Conglomerate.

Tiger's destination was home to The Deep Jungle.

15 – THE CELEBRATION IN THE DEEP JUNGLE

Much later, in The Deep Jungle, there was a celebration. Not far from Tiger's home all the animals had come together for a mass party. The music was provided by a wide range of animals and insects with string music performed by a group of crickets using one leg bent against the other. Gorilla and his monkey friends were on percussion, they used two hollow coconuts and put a thin layer of skin (no one asked where the skin came from) over each one to provide some bongo drums. Joining the band were some frogs who would croak in tune. To be fair the noise was not that bad and there was even talk from the usually angry Gorilla of the band going on tour throughout The Jungle, performing at will. Gorilla did mention that they needed a female vocalist but no one was brave enough to ask Tiger, even in a state of euphoria.

In front of the band, rabbits were dancing, birds were flapping their wings. Donkey, Jim and Jill were hugging and very happy. In front of the dancing was a large fire fuelled by wood with a barbeque on top of it in the form of a spit. There was some meat on there and to the side of the barbeque some fruit and fresh vegetables. Dino was sat right in front of the barbeque munching hard.

"Sorry Leopard," said Dino as Leopard approached him, "I'm back on the meat! This greenery doesn't sit very well with me," Dino said. Leopard walked away leaving Dino to his feast and the animals to celebrate.

Just outside of the celebrations, through some bramble and bushes, Foxy leant up against a tree on his hind legs looking on. It had been a tough few days for Foxy, now he was stripped down, devoid of his combat armour and was just back to his normal self. Foxy was very tired and the last couple of days had had an effect on him. His tail was now just bone with no fur, a part of his ear was missing and he was bruised. At least the bruises will heal, Foxy thought. Tiger walked through the bramble, Foxy spotted her with Crow on her shoulder. Tiger whispered something to Crow and Crow flew away, for once not squawking with voice.

"Foxy," Tiger said.

"Tiger," replied Foxy, as Tiger sat down.

"What are you doing out here Foxy? Why aren't you celebrating? You're not leaving us, are you?"

"It's time to go Tiger. I thought I'd make a quiet exit while everyone was celebrating," said Foxy sincerely, not trying to outfox Tiger.

"But Foxy, this is all of your doing. You pioneered this plan, you saved us all!" Tiger exclaimed, surprised at Foxy's behaviour.

"No Tiger. You did," replied Foxy.

"We did it then," compromised Tiger. "But, Foxy, at what cost? Your tail, your ear, your home? All this for me and the animals?"

"If I didn't try, the cost would've been my soul Tiger," Foxy said with his front legs and paws extended to explain to Tiger.

"Yes, yes, Foxy is right," Tiger said and Foxy jumped up and kissed Tiger on her whiskers making her cheeks go the colour of fresh beetroot. "I want to thank you Foxy for making me stand up for what's important," she said.

"Hey, don't mention it Tiger. It was Foxy Power!" Foxy smiled and winked at Tiger.

"Cocky Foxy," Tiger said and smiled back. Foxy fell on all fours and took a step back and smiled at Tiger, turned and walked off.

"Bye," Foxy said as he strolled off. Tiger called after him when was a few yards away.

"Where're you going Foxy?" Tiger enquired.

"Home," Foxy replied, "I'm going home." He carried on walking out of The Deep Jungle to another part of The Jungle to find a new home and almost certainly a new adventure or two.

Foxy Power.

Foxy will return in –
Foxy Tales: Contagion

Printed in Poland
by Amazon Fulfillment
Poland Sp. z o.o., Wrocław